"You shoul

D0205802

Alex had thought about leaving. The old Alex would have been long gone days ago. Still, he couldn't.

He saw it, then, in her eyes. JJ was waiting for him to leave. Watching for him to betray her in the way she had been betrayed before.

"I can't leave."

"Why?"

"You really don't know the answer to that?"

Her face flushed. "Why would I ask a question I know the answer to?"

JJ tried hard not to look him in the eye, but the more she dodged him, the stronger his conviction became. "Because I'm supposed to stay." And then, even though it felt like jumping off a cliff to do so, Alex made himself add, "And because I want to stay."

Her eyes widened, and she backed up. "Max doesn't need you."

"I'm not staying for Max." He reached for her hand.

At first JJ edged out of his grasp, but when he took another step, she stilled her hand and let him grasp it. "I'm staying for you."

Books by Allie Pleiter

Love Inspired

My So-Called Love Life
The Perfect Blend
**Bluegrass Hero*
**Bluegrass Courtship*
**Bluegrass Blessings*
**Bluegrass Christmas*
Easter Promises
*"Bluegrass Easter"
†*Falling for the Fireman*
†*The Fireman's Homecoming*
†*The Firefighter's Match*

Love Inspired Historical

Masked by Moonlight
Mission of Hope
Yukon Wedding
Homefront Hero
Family Lessons

Love Inspired Single Title

Bad Heiress Day
Queen Esther & the Second Graders of Doom

*Kentucky Corners
†Gordon Falls

ALLIE PLEITER

Enthusiastic but slightly untidy mother of two, RITA® Award finalist Allie Pleiter writes both fiction and nonfiction. An avid knitter and unreformed chocoholic, she spends her days writing books, drinking coffee and finding new ways to avoid housework. Allie grew up in Connecticut, holds a B.S. in speech from Northwestern University and spent fifteen years in the field of professional fund-raising. She lives with her husband, children and a Havanese dog named Bella in the suburbs of Chicago, Illinois.

The Firefighter's Match

Allie Pleiter

If you purchased this book without a cover you should be aware that this book is stolen property. It was reported as "unsold and destroyed" to the publisher, and neither the author nor the publisher has received any payment for this "stripped book."

Recycling programs for this product may not exist in your area.

ISBN-13: 978-0-373-81728-3

THE FIREFIGHTER'S MATCH

Copyright © 2013 by Alyse Stanko Pleiter

All rights reserved. Except for use in any review, the reproduction or utilization of this work in whole or in part in any form by any electronic, mechanical or other means, now known or hereafter invented, including xerography, photocopying and recording, or in any information storage or retrieval system, is forbidden without the written permission of the editorial office, Love Inspired Books, 233 Broadway, New York, NY 10279 U.S.A.

This is a work of fiction. Names, characters, places and incidents are either the product of the author's imagination or are used fictitiously, and any resemblance to actual persons, living or dead, business establishments, events or locales is entirely coincidental.

This edition published by arrangement with Love Inspired Books.

® and TM are trademarks of Love Inspired Books, used under license. Trademarks indicated with ® are registered in the United States Patent and Trademark Office, the Canadian Trade Marks Office and in other countries.

www.Harlequin.com

Printed in U.S.A.

And we know that in all things God works for the good of those who love Him, who have been called according to his purpose.

—*Romans* 8:28

Dedication:

To Rachel
Who has overcome so much

Acknowledgments:

This story needed a hefty dose of technical support to get the details right. My thanks to fire chief Don Lay for again checking all the firefighter and firehouse facts. Lisa Rosen and Dr. David Chen from the Rehabilitation Institute of Chicago were also great helps. Thanks as well to Sean Smith, who lent me his climbing knowledge and expertise. If any of the medical, climbing or firefighting facts of this book are incorrect, the fault lies with me and not with any of these generous experts.

Chapter One

Gordon Falls, Illinois

1:48 a.m.

2:36 a.m.

3:14 in the why-on-earth-can't-a-soul-get-to-sleep morning and JJ Jones still lay as wide-eyed as if she had downed a quartet of espresso drinks.

Refusing to lie there one more minute under the false pretense of drowsiness, JJ reached for an elastic band. She pulled her long blond hair back into a resolute ponytail and stepped into a pair of jeans under her oversize T-shirt. Padding to the not-yet-familiar kitchen of her rental cottage, JJ let the summer evening breeze coming off the Gordon River soothe her annoyance.

It was a lovely place, even in the middle of the

night. She could almost count her insomnia as a pleasantry here, the nights were so enjoyable.

She grinned at her brother's handwriting, still sloppy in his brief set of "Guest Instructions" taped to the refrigerator door. They were mostly useless items with a few wisecracks like "#6. Don't drown in the river," and "#8. Go to the hospital if you get bitten by something you can't identify." Max ran his cottage and boat rental businesses like he ran the rest of his life: at breakneck speed with little thought to useful details. His talent at haphazard messes was one of the reasons she'd opted to stay in a rental cottage rather than Max's grubby house.

She addressed the list, stained in three spots and taped back together in one corner. "I've seen your house. I've seen your life. You'd have lasted eight seconds in my unit, Max. Six, tops."

It felt foolish to chastise an empty room, but since leaving the army a month ago she'd not yet learned how to be comfortably alone. That was why she was here: to reacquaint herself with the virtues of peace and privacy. To ease her way into settling down in Gordon Falls alongside her brother. And, if she was truly honest, to get the chronic knot out of her stomach and squelch the nonstop urge to look over her shoulder. Helping Max out by tending to his business for a month while he was off on yet another of his crazy schemes was just a temporary way to pay the bills while she got her life in order.

JJ laughed at her own thoughts. Who was she kidding? Picking up after Max's multiple fiascoes was a lifetime gig. Jones River Sports was just this year's verse to the same old song. She was amazed, actually, that he'd held on to the business as long as he had. The real surprise, though, was that she was actually enjoying the benefits that came with this particular scheme. JJ liked the location and thought she might really want to stay, even when Max pulled up stakes, as he was sure to someday do.

Pushing past the diet sodas on the fridge's top shelf, JJ found a bowl of grapes and was pulling them out to snack on when she heard a tune coming in the window. She turned, not quite able to place the melody or the instrument. It was an instrument being played outside, wasn't it? Not someone's nearby radio? A sour note, followed by a second attempt at a melody, confirmed her guess. It wasn't a guitar, and it wasn't a violin, either. A banjo? No, a ukulele. She set the bowl down on the yellow Formica counter and peered out the window. It was. It was a ukulele. People still played those? In the middle of the night?

She popped a grape into her mouth and squinted harder in the direction of the dock. Max had said something about a crazy renter, some guy who paid cash in advance through a broker and wouldn't give a name. She'd never have rented to someone acting that suspicious, but of course Max thought that was all great fun.

"Just don't bug him and he probably won't murder you." That had been Max's final instruction on the mystery renter. The creepy, nocturnal mystery renter.

Yet how creepy could a guy be who launched into a bad rendition of "When You Wish Upon A Star" at—she checked the clock with a grimace—3:21 a.m.?

Taking the big walking stick Max had given her as a parting gift, JJ slipped into her sandals to go find out.

She worked her way down the path toward the figure of a man sitting on the dock, his silhouette crisp against the yellow wedge of light thrown by the dock's single bulb. Given the circumstances, JJ couldn't decide whether to be grateful or annoyed that she gave the entire scene a military assessment before coming closer. Trying to ease up on the military vigilance didn't mean throwing caution to the wind. This could be a potentially dangerous situation. People were weird, even out here in tiny Illinois tourist towns. And let's face it—normal people don't croon…"White Christmas" now, at 3:30 a.m. in July.

She stepped on a squeaky board and the man turned, still strumming a chord. He was her age, which surprised her. His profile was rugged, with a tumble of sandy-blond waves that were overdue for a cut. He wore one of those high-tech outdoorsman shirts but a ragged pair of jeans, and an expensive-looking watch glinted from his wrist. Could murderous psychopaths afford fine timepieces? Her military vigilance answered that: people can make themselves look like anything.

"It's July," she said, not knowing how else to address this kook.

"It's snowing in New Zealand."

"That still doesn't make it time for Christmas carols."

He went back to "When You Wish Upon a Star." "I'm sorry I woke you." He had a remarkably interesting voice—rich and deep, like a radio announcer but without all the theatricality.

"You didn't, actually. Wake me, I mean. I was up."

He shifted to face her and the light shone on his features. He looked like someone out of an outdoor magazine—handsome and carefree. "Another night owl?" She was startled by the friendliness in his words. He gave off the attitude of a man who played hard: rumpled, almost unkempt, but with loads of energy. A bit like Max but without the rough, destructive edges.

"Not by choice." She started to say more, about how being up at night was often an asset in the military, but stopped herself because she knew nothing about this guy. She shouldn't offer extra information to a stranger, even to make conversation. She wasn't used to even wanting to make conversation. It certainly wasn't the appropriate response to have to a potential sociopath.

He smiled—a dynamic, engaging smile that made it hard not to smile back—and switched to an ethnic-sounding tune she didn't recognize. An owl hooted from somewhere behind her and she heard a fish jump from the river beyond him. "Been up nights since I was in college, myself. Still, I can never sleep past the sunrise even if I do manage to doze off."

He nodded toward the instrument. "That's a Himalayan lullaby. The lady who taught it to me swore it worked, but I've never had much success."

New Zealand, Himalayan mountains—the upscale gear was starting to make sense. It was easy to be carefree if you had the funds to play like that, especially at his age. He doubled back to a few bars of "White Christmas," evidently tiring of the lullaby. She decided to try an experiment—after all, this guy had no idea she knew any of the information Max had told her. "Who are you?"

He hesitated only a moment before answering, "Bing Crosby, of course."

"You are not Bing Crosby."

"I had an Amazonian tribal chief tell me I had the soul of a monkey, but I'm not that, either."

Given what she'd seen of his personality, she had a feeling it was actually a better guess than Bing Crosby. She ought to introduce herself, force his hand, but JJ found she didn't want to. It was part fear—after all, no one knew anything about this guy other than he was well traveled and had deep pockets—and part to keep things private. Gordon Falls was still a bit of a hiding place for her. She was new enough that almost no one in town knew her past. This dock was no place to start creating unwanted conversations about what the war was like and why she wasn't over there any longer. "Does that make me Judy Garland?" For as many nights as she stayed up watching television, she ought to have a better knowledge of old movies.

"Bing's" smile doubled, and the man's eyes fairly glowed. "Actually, I think that makes you Rosemary Clooney."

JJ laughed. It felt foreign but not altogether bad. "I could do worse."

He held her gaze for a moment before replying, "So could I." A few chords went by before he asked, "So, Rosemary, what keeps you up at night?"

There was one of those loaded questions she'd hoped to avoid. "Too much to think about, I suppose."

His sigh echoed across the water. "Oh, I know that tune. I suppose if we really were Bing and Rosemary, we'd be counting our blessings instead of sheep. Isn't that how the song in the movie goes?"

"I have no idea." She sat down on the little wooden bench that ran along the side of the dock. Being up in the middle of the night was always such a lonely thing; it was nice to have a little company.

He looked up and she followed his gaze. The summer sky was a sapphire blanket studded with stars, a glorious display. One of the benefits of being such a raging insomniac was that she got to see a lot of magnificent stars. It was nearly four; the first ribbons of pink sunrise were beginning to pour pastel colors into the night sky. The mystery man gave a little whistle of appreciation as if he'd had the same thought. "I gotta wonder, Rosemary, how many people slog through life never watching the amazing spectacle of the sun coming up?"

JJ laughed again. "Why, Bing, you sound like some kind of commercial."

He gave a soft laugh of his own, but JJ noticed an edge to his amusement. "It's sort of what I do. Or did. Or maybe still do."

It was crystal clear to JJ that whatever "Bing" really did, it was a sore spot. "Which is…?"

He shook his head. "Not here. The whole point of being here is to be far away from all that."

JJ could understand that longing to just get away from it all. Wasn't the bone-deep craving to disappear the whole reason she was here in Gordon Falls? This man wanted peace and privacy just as much as she did. It wouldn't be fair to call that a psychotic impulse, even if he was a bit odd. Intriguing, but definitely odd.

The first bird of morning called out across the water, and JJ stifled a welcome yawn. "Well, good night, Mr. Crosby."

"White Christmas" wafted across the water again, a joke for the fish in the middle of July. "Good morning, Miss Clooney. Sweet dreams." He turned back to the river and hummed softly as he played, as comfortable as if he'd lived there his whole life.

No one had said that to her in years, since being tucked into bed by her father back when she was small. It struck her in a close and unsettling way. "Yeah," she blurted out, absolutely unwilling to say "You, too," or any other such too-friendly reply. Now she was glad he didn't know her name. It felt like he knew too much already.

The next night, the Beatles song "Yesterday" came in through the window just as the sun was going down. While part of her resisted, another part of her yearned to accept the musical invitation to join him on the dock. This time on the river was the opposite of everything she'd wanted to leave behind in Afghanistan, and while she couldn't yet say why, "Bing" had become a part of that escape.

It reminded JJ of something she'd almost forgotten: that a good kind of scared existed. A person could be anxious about something good just as much as she could be terrified of something bad.

Just as she had that novel thought, the old cautions seemed to roar up with twice their strength. *You know nothing about him. Clever strangers can seem all too friendly.*

She stood there, listening to the music, trying to decide what to do, when she caught her reflection in the darkened window. JJ didn't like what she saw.

Are you going to go through life like this? On guard? Waiting for trouble? Or are you going to choose to heal?

"I could probably knock him out—or knock him into the water—if he tried anything." JJ startled herself by addressing her reflection aloud. She really was a little too freaked out at being alone these days.

Well, the music from the dock seemed to say that she should go make some new friends.

Alex Cushman stared at the path that led down to the dock, willing her to appear.

The goal of coming out here was to find some solitude, to spend time figuring out the new direction his life would take. Last night, that new direction had taken an impulsive detour.

He shouldn't have been surprised. Impulsive detours were, after all, an Alex Cushman specialty.

Tonight he'd brought a small clay fire pit out on the dock. The temptation of chocolate, graham crackers, two sticks and some marshmallows? Well, that was another classic Cushman impulse. It was one he'd wanted to share with his mystery lady. The anonymity they'd had last night transfixed him somehow. He didn't know her name, and she didn't know his. This trip was supposed to let him step out of Alex Cushman's skin for a while, to lay down the frustrations and complications of who he was so he could figure out who he was supposed to be. Now that he'd met her, he didn't want to escape alone. *Come on, Lord, this had to be Your doing, so bring her back tonight. There's something about her.*

Just as he was finishing the last bars of the Beatles tune and pondering how many s'mores a grown man could eat alone and not look pathetic, Alex heard footsteps. And there she was.

"Rosemary" wasn't anything like the kind of women who'd caught his eye back in Denver. He doubted most of his friends would call her pretty, but she had this extraordinary strength about her: a hardened, warrior quality. He found himself wondering if she softened her appearance by wearing makeup or jewelry during the day—after all, they had met in the middle of the night. Somehow, he doubted it. He got the sense that appearing soft or approachable was the last thing she wanted.

She was also way too lean—someone ought to hand her a few quarts of ice cream and coax her into gaining some pounds. Maybe that's where the stupid s'mores idea had come from.

"Hungry?" he asked, putting down the ukulele and picking up one of the two small sticks.

She raised a skeptical eyebrow. "S'mores?"

"It sounded clever when I thought of it." Alex offered. "Now it's feeling a bit, well, dumb." He extended the second stick to her. "The only thing that will feel dumber is if I'm forced to eat these alone."

"Mr. Crosby," she said, narrowing one eye but taking another step toward him. "You're a little odd, you know that?"

"If you were listening, tonight I'm Paul." Alex tore open the package of graham crackers and began snapping them into squares before she could decline his invitation.

"I'm not going to be John, George or Ringo." She was trying to make a joke of it, but there was an edge to her voice that let him know she didn't trust this little game one bit.

"Hey," he said softly, "you don't have to be anybody." Alex skewered a marshmallow and held it over the small fire. "I'm a torch 'em guy myself. I like my marshmallows in flames."

He'd meant it to be funny, but a darkness flashed over her fair features at his words. It didn't take a marketing genius to see she was out here to get away from something as much as he was. Something to do with fire—or just danger in general? Maybe. And really, was that so much of a stretch? Why else did people rent tiny cabins out on the river if not to get away from their problems?

For a minute, Alex thought she was going to turn around and leave, and he'd be sitting there, trying to figure out how he'd just insulted a woman with a single marshmallow. She was thinking about it; he could see it in her face. After a long moment, she pulled a marshmallow from the bag and positioned it on the end of her stick with entirely too much precision. "Golden brown," she said. "No charring, just gooey."

She sat down, hugging her knees to her chest as she held the stick over the orange embers.

"I'm Alex." The words jumped out of his mouth of their own accord, shocking even him.

Her eyes flashed up toward him, wide with surprise before they narrowed again. "Alex for real?"

The question held an inexplicable weight. "Alex for real." He felt exposed for no reason. He stared at her, wondering if she'd share her own name. Any such wondering was squelched when his marshmallow burst into flames, a tiny black torch burning against the darkening sky.

"JJ," she said as he blew it out. The thing was too burned, even for him, but he knew he'd eat it anyway. Alex wondered if he'd ever know what JJ stood for or why such a thing should matter to him at all.

"You're not really going to eat that, are you?" Behind her scowl was the barest hint of a smile.

"Blackened. The best kind." Alex smacked his lips for emphasis as he squished the lava-like confection between the cracker and chocolate. "Savory." He bit into it, tasting nothing but burned sugar. "And crunchy."

JJ assembled hers with the attention of a chef. She ate it just as carefully, in strategic bites, whereas he'd just stuffed the whole thing into this mouth in one gooey-black splurge.

"You're a careful person, aren't you, JJ?"

She bit another precise corner off with an assessing glance. "You're not."

They went on for hours. Talking about little things—ice cream flavors, whether or not barista coffee was really worth the cost—and big things—why nature calmed the soul, what was going to happen to little places like Gordon Falls, why the high school version of who'd they'd be when they grew up had proved to be nothing close to the truth. The subjects seem to go deeper as the last traces of sunlight faded. Without ever speaking of it, they'd come to some sort of no-detail pact between them. No last names, no careers, none of that stuff. Wonderfully, effortlessly mysterious. A dark, luminescent bubble in the middle of nowhere.

"Alex," JJ began, and he found himself wallowing in how she said his name, "why are you here?"

That could require another six hours of conversation. How do you explain being confounded by success, losing focus when focus was once your stock and trade? Really, what kind of person gets weary of their own supposed genius? Part of him was ready to spill it all, and part of him felt like he'd emptied out half his soul already. "I'm trying to figure out why it doesn't all fit together anymore and what to do about it." It was true, but nowhere near the full of it. He was here to figure out if he had to lay down Adventure Gear, the business he'd once loved and now hated. Only he couldn't tell her that. To speak it out loud would bring that mess here, and he wanted all those problems to stay far away.

He looked at her, pleased to feel so startlingly close to her despite not even knowing her last name—or even what JJ stood for. "Why are *you* here?"

She sighed and looked out over the water. It was now full dark, and a perfect crescent moon cast sparkles on the water where she swished one foot into the river. "Because I don't feel like I belong anywhere else. Anywhere at all, actually."

He laughed softly.

She scowled. "It's not so funny, you know."

"No, it's just that I've felt like I belong everywhere for so long, that actually sounds nice. I know it's not—I mean, not for you—but isn't it crazy how God skews the world for each of us?"

JJ hugged her knee again and propped her

chin up, looking childlike and elegant at the same time. "So you believe in God, huh?"

Alex leaned back on his elbows and took in the glory of the sky. "I've seen so many amazing parts of the world that I can't help but know He's there. The big, grand creation stuff has always been easy for me to believe in." He rolled his head to catch JJ's eye. "It's the up close and personal stuff that seems to have come unraveled lately. I'm not a guy who does well with questions and doubts." He was grateful she didn't ask for an explanation.

After a long pause, JJ offered, "I did, once. Believe, I mean." Her voice was quiet, almost weary. "At least I thought I did."

"And then?" He rolled over so that he was on his side facing her. She was fascinating. There wasn't another word for it. Alex felt like he could stay up and talk out here for weeks.

"And then I saw too many things that made it hard to keep believing." He knew not to press for anything further, but some part of him was grateful when, after a long pause, she added, "I was in the war."

It explained so much. Her hard edges, the way her eyes assessed things, the weariness that seemed to inhabit every part of her. Suddenly every response he could think of sounded trite and placating.

"Yep," she said, twice as wearily as before. "It's always a fabulous conversation killer."

"No, it's just…"

"Please." JJ held up a hand. "I'm so used to it by now. I've heard all the standard required replies and silence is actually a nice change."

"I don't know how you come back from something like that." His own weariness, how globetrotting for adventure had lost its luster seemed downright ridiculous now.

"I suppose that makes two of us." She got up to leave.

Alex scrambled upright. "Don't. Please don't go like that. Not now." Her eyes looked a thousand miles deep, boring into Alex the way they did right now. "Two minutes. Just stay two more minutes."

She stayed two more hours, still lingering when it started to rain. They got past the awkwardness, settling into a companionship that was as startling as it was soothing. Even soaked to the skin, it was the best night of his life.

Chapter Two

Worst day of my life.

Alex let that thought sink in as he raised his hand to knock on her cottage door two nights later. Sure, he could have called—the office had given him her cell number—but this wasn't the kind of news that ought to be delivered over the phone. *I owe Josephine Jones the dignity of hearing about this face to face.* Now he knew her full name and was stunningly sorry he did. *It's going to be awful. In so many ways.*

He knew she'd be up despite the excruciatingly early hour. In the days since they'd met, he had come to adore her insomnia with as much strength as he had once hated his. It was a terrible thing to lose the ability to sleep when the rest of the world could. Until JJ, he'd cursed his night-owl tendencies. For the past days, he had welcomed them.

Alex had checked the dock before heading up the gravel path that led to her house. He'd tried to tell himself that he was hoping to find her there because the peaceful surroundings might soften the hard news he carried. But he knew that wasn't the real reason why he'd gone to the dock. He had taken the time down there to gather his own composure, to pray for the right words.

Finally, he'd realized there were no right words. Not for this kind of news. There was no easy way to admit to her what he knew, who he was, how much of the blame for this tragic news he was bringing her could be laid at his own feet.

I asked You to show me why I shouldn't leave Adventure Gear behind, Lord. Did You have to show me this way?

He rapped gently on the cottage door, cringing as the light came on in the window he knew was her kitchen. It was still early enough for the moon to be hanging close and delicate in the brightening sky.

She opened the door with a yawning smile. "Hey. A bit early, even for you."

He still couldn't figure out how JJ exuded such a powerful, unusual beauty to him. So different from the usual frills and baubles. The difference struck him again as he stared at her, even as regret cut a sharp edge into his gut. *She'll probably hate me by the end of today. Maybe even by the end of this conversation.*

"This can't wait. May I come in?"

She had every right to look baffled. They'd both been out here for solitude, and though a friendship had begun to grow between them, they had kept out of each other's private lives by mutual intuition. Really, it was the most amazing thing he'd ever known, this odd relationship he had with JJ. Their no-details pact had spawned the most powerful and deep conversations. Nature did that—pulled people into a bubble that shut out the mundane world. Alex had spent a career capitalizing on the natural world's ability to heal a person's spirit.

Only now it was coming back to slap him in the face. Hard.

"Um…sure. I can put some coffee on or something."

They probably wouldn't have time for coffee once he gave her the news. Alex was pretty sure he'd already taken more time than was wise, fishing fruitlessly for some kinder way to deliver the facts he came to share. "Don't bother. But you need to sit down. I've…um… I've got a few things to tell you."

JJ yanked her blond ponytail tighter—a habit of hers, he'd discovered—and led them into the kitchen. It had the sparse, uniform quality of a rental property, but he could see bits of JJ's personality in the crock of flowers sitting in the middle of the table and a few other touches. All he knew was that she was here for the summer—he hadn't even learned why until the call from his brother, Sam, had come. Had he known her last name, he might have made the connection to her brother and steered clear of those blue eyes. At the moment that little detail felt like a cruel joke God had played.

"What is going on?"

"My name is Alex Cushman."

"Hey, wait, why are you telling me your last name? I thought we…"

Alex kept going, plowing through this before it hurt more. "My brother is Sam Cushman. Together we own Adventure Gear."

Her brows furrowed. She hadn't yet put together why that mattered, but it only took a few seconds before she said, "The sporting equipment company?"

"We supply equipment to the television show *Wide Wild World*."

Her eyes widened. If she'd been sleepy before, she was wide-awake now. "The reality competition show? Where Max is?"

"Where Max is."

"But wait, I never told you about Max. How do you know all...?" Her features sharpened instantly. "Wait...what's going on? Why are you here?"

"There's been an accident on the set of the show. Involving Max. I'm here to take you to the hospital because it's pretty serious." *Pretty serious.* He'd had to think for five minutes to come up with the right words to walk her up to the reality of what had happened to Max Jones.

Her hands covered her face for an instant, then went back down to fist in her lap. "He's okay?"

Alex tried to keep his voice level and calm. He'd really hoped to avoid that question. "No, Max is not okay, but he survived and we're arranging for him to get the best of care as fast as we can. That means you ought to pull a few things together and come with me. They've taken him into Chicago by helicopter, and we've got one waiting for you and me over in Dubuque. If you have parents who ought to come, give me that information and I'll pass it along to the studio to arrange travel."

"Mom doesn't know?"

"Max only listed you on his emergency info. I didn't know you were Max's sister until about thirty minutes ago. I'm sorry."

JJ shot off the chair. "Of course Max left Mom out of the loop. He's *fabulous* at that." The split-second frustration was quickly replaced with teary-eyed worry. "What happened to him?"

Alex had decided to parcel out the details of the accident in small stages, giving JJ time to cope with the catastrophe. Catastrophe. That was one of Sam's favorite words, one Alex usually banned from his vocabulary—but it fit this time.

"Max fell during a night climb."

"Fell? Far?"

"Yes. He was airlifted in serious but stable condition to Lincoln General about twenty minutes ago." He was hoping that would be enough, that she would take those facts and move forward to gather her things. She didn't budge. "JJ, we should go as soon as we can."

He saw something click behind her eyes. She shifted gears into a harder, more precise version of herself, but she still didn't get up. Instead, her eyes narrowed at Alex as she watched him more closely. Of course. She'd mentioned she was planning to use her experience to join the volunteer fire department here if she stayed. She wasn't just a soldier—she must have been a first responder of some kind. She wasn't going to let him off with a vague assessment of Max's condition. Her eyes told him she needed as much information as he could give right now, no matter how bad.

"They suspect a spinal cord injury. He's not conscious, and they're going to keep him sedated while they assess the…" he hesitated to use this word but knew it was what she was looking for "…damage. Lincoln General has the best doctors for this. The show's producers are doing all they can but right now we really should go."

She'd been too calm up to this point. The women he knew would have lost it ten minutes ago, would be rushing in tears to the car he had outside. JJ was pulling herself inward, winding up into a tight ball of control. It worried him more than tears would, especially knowing what he did about why she was in Gordon Falls. She'd come here to escape the tension and turmoil she'd known overseas, and he'd literally brought trauma to her doorstep.

He'd almost breathed a sigh of relief when she turned toward the hallway, hopefully to gather her things. He went to make a call to the office for an update but stopped when she turned at the end of the room to glare at him with ice-cold eyes. "You're Alex Cushman. You own Adventure Gear and you're involved with the show *WWW* where Max just practically got himself killed."

It was an excruciatingly fair assessment of the circumstances. Alex could only nod.

She made a disgusted sound that Alex felt in the pit of his stomach and left the room.

JJ had ridden in helicopters more times than she could count. She'd done things—seen things—that would make most people run in fear. Serving as a firefighter in Afghanistan had given her nerves of steel.

Or so she'd thought. As the helicopter swooped up off the ground and veered east toward Chicago, a sick sense of dread filled her. She'd been in enough crises to pick up on everything Alex wasn't saying. Worry about her brother battled with anger at herself for feeling so disappointed in the man Alex had turned out to be. The dreamy bubble she'd cast around this stranger, this man who had captured her imagination, had now burst in the worst way possible.

When had she lost her common sense? Their

avoidance of everyday topics, deliberately not sharing their identities… All that seemed beyond foolhardy now. Ordinarily, JJ was nothing if not careful.

Unlike Max. Max was a carnival of carelessness. Suddenly the jokes Mom and her late father would make, like, "It's a wonder Max hasn't gotten himself killed yet," weren't so funny. A wave of concern for her younger brother waged war with anger over having to deal with another Max-induced calamity. She leaned her head against the aircraft's cool glass in an effort to calm her roiling stomach.

"Are you going to be okay?" Everything about Alex had shifted in the past hour. He'd lost the casual air, that look of having all the time in the world that had first drawn her to his silhouette as he sat on the dock in the moonlight. Now, even over the chopping of the helicopter blades, his voice was clipped and tight. The unmistakable tone of someone trying to manage a crisis.

"I doubt it." She wasn't going to give Mr. Adventure Gear the satisfaction of an "I'll be fine." Nothing about this was going to be fine, at least not anytime soon. A man's mother isn't hauled in from out of state for small injuries. Damaged spinal cords didn't heal completely, if ever. She looked at him and leaned in. "Tell me what you know."

"There's not much to know just yet."

Standard first-responder jargon. "Tell me all the stuff you haven't told me yet. I'm not going to go to pieces." Alex's eyes told her he feared just that. Other people probably would in this situation. Only she wasn't other people. "Look," she tried again, although shouting over the helicopter noise didn't exactly make for easy chatting. "I'd feel better with more facts." *And less coddling,* she added silently.

Alex raked his fingers through his hair. "They were rappelling down the side of a cliff. Darkness, bats, all kinds of good television. Evidently you earned bonus points if you went first because no one knew what was at the bottom, and Max jumped at the chance to increase his lead. He'd been the clear front-runner all week."

"I had no idea, but then again, how could I? You don't allow me any communication with Max." Technically, it was the show that didn't allow communication—Max had shown her the pile of "do not disclose" statements he'd had to sign before the car had come to pick him up. She knew it wasn't fair to blame Alex for what *WWW* had done, but the panic was yelling accusations in the back of her brain she didn't have the energy to fight. "I didn't even know he was in the state park…so close."

"You weren't supposed to know. The only reason I knew was because it was my job to make sure equipment got there. I'm not even sure Max knew he was only an hour from home. They do a good job of isolating the set."

He was skirting the issue. "So what happened?"

"He fell. We think he may have swatted a bat and taken his hand off the break strand—I don't know the details yet, really—but he swung far to one side and hit the platform where the camera crew was." She watched Alex pause for a moment, crafting his next words. "His back struck the metal scaffolding."

"Was he wearing safety gear?" Max was in the habit of skipping such equipment. In the week before he left, as he was teaching her how to rent the kayaks and canoes he offered alongside cabin and motorboat rentals, she watched him give a safety lesson five times a day to customers, then completely disregard all of it when he went out himself.

"Yes, he was. The show required it. I don't think I've heard mention of any head injuries, although he wasn't conscious when they lifted him. I do know he…hit…pretty hard. I'll check my phone again when we land but I don't think they really have a lot of information. I don't want to tell you something I can't be sure is true."

"Yeah." JJ fought the gruesome image of Max's limp body being pulled from the rigging. She kept reminding herself he was still alive. But how close to death and for how long?

"Hey." Alex's hand landed softly on her shoulder. "I'm really sorry this happened. I'm praying for Max."

"Sure." The past hour's revelations were ambushing her composure, stealing her sense of control when she needed it most. She had been just as guilty of not divulging personal information during their long dock conversations as Alex had been, but somehow it all felt like hiding to her now. Her head knew Alex hadn't deliberately hidden his connection with *WWW* any more than she'd deliberately hidden her combat tour, but her gut felt cheated. Lied to, deceived, blindsided.

"They texted me just before we took off to say Max was going into surgery. You won't be able to see him when we get there, but you should be able to when he wakes up." He pulled out his phone to scroll down and reread the message, then looked up at her, his face cast in orange by the sunrise in front of them. "Although they are going to keep him under heavy sedation for the next twenty-four hours."

"A medically induced coma." JJ wasn't a doctor, but she'd been near enough medic units to know that didn't call for a lot of optimism.

"They didn't use those words, but I'd guess yes." She watched him choose to share the next fact, able to read the reluctance on his face. "The spinal cord injury is far enough up that they are worried about the use of his arms. I want you to believe me, JJ, when I say we are working with the studio to bring the very best people in on this. He'll have the best care available—I promise you that."

She couldn't find much comfort in that. In Afghanistan, she'd seen burn victims given "the very best care available." It only meant their lives were ten percent less excruciating. That didn't seem like much of an advantage.

Alex checked his watch. "We should be there in twenty minutes."

Her mind turned back to the secrets he had kept from her. Now all of his upscale toys made sense. His shoes were top of the line; his leather bag looked like it had cost more than her first car. It was logical that he'd own the best of his store's merchandise, but it suddenly filled her with resentment. She was finding out something new about Alex Cushman every minute, and that didn't feel good at all. "But you don't work for *WWW.* Why are you here and not them?"

That seemed to catch him off guard. He thought for a moment before answering. "Because it was the right thing to do. I was nearby and I knew you. I didn't think you should hear this news from a stranger."

The irony of his words struck them both at the same time. He *was* a stranger. She knew Alex—she'd been startled, almost frightened by how familiar he felt out there on the dock—but she didn't *know* him.

"I'm not a stranger, JJ." He'd sensed what she was thinking. "I'm so, so sorry this happened but I'm glad I have the chance to be here to help you and your family."

Corporate sorry—the "don't sue me" kind of sorry—wasn't anything close to the kind of sorry that would make up for the impact this would have on Max's life. Even if he survived his injuries, he'd be dealing with the consequences for months. Maybe even years. People didn't just get up and walk away from spinal cord injuries. Max's life as he knew it might very well be over. "Sorry" didn't come close to covering that.

Alex grabbed her hand. "Hey, I know you're upset. You have every right to be. But please don't cast me as the enemy right now. I'm here and I want to help and I'm going to help. I'll make sure Adventure Gear and *WWW* take responsibility for whatever happened and make it right. I want you to believe that I'm not just spouting some company line here. I truly do care about what happens to you and your brother. I'm still just Alex."

JJ pulled her hand from his. "No, you're not."

Chapter Three

The panic in his brother's voice was getting annoying. "This could be a publicity nightmare, Alex. You need to get back to Denver and hold down the fort while I stay here on the set. I talked to the guard station an hour ago and he told me there was an *Entertainment Today* reporter sniffing around. The studio's not containing it—for all I know they want it to leak to give the show more publicity. Some of these production assistants are too young not to fall for a reporter flashing a wad of cash for spilling the details."

Alex leaned onto the cold hospital cafeteria table and rested his head in his hand. It didn't feel like there was enough coffee in the world to get him through today. "Sam, they just airlifted a contestant to a trauma center. It won't take long for people to figure out there's been an accident."

"I want to keep a lid on things for a few days at least. I just hope the *WWW* execs are good at this kind of damage control." Since the beginning of their association with *Wide Wild World,* Sam had an annoying habit of counting himself among the studio types. It was one of the reasons Alex steered clear of any involvement in this promotional deal, compromising instead with a quick product delivery and a "vacation nearby."

"Let them handle it, Sam. We're just a vendor. I stepped in to help with JJ because I was nearby, but the heavy lifting on this belongs to them."

There was a brief, uncomfortable pause before his brother said, "Not entirely."

Alex squeezed his eyes shut. In the seven years he and his brother had built Adventure Gear into a serious player in the outdoor equipment market, nothing good had ever come after Sam's use of the phrase "not entirely." "What are you saying?"

"We don't really know what happened yet."

"Of course we don't know. Max Jones isn't even out of surgery. It'll be hours before we know what's going on. If then." Alex's stomach twisted as he remembered the look in JJ's eyes as the doctor had explained the situation. There were so many unknowns at this point, and JJ didn't strike him as the type to handle ambiguity well.

"I don't mean with Jones. I mean with the fall."

"That's what those stunt production guys are for. It's their job to solve those kinds of problems before they happen. And right now, it's their job to figure out where they went wrong. I really think you need to keep out of this as much as you can, Sam. We don't need to get mixed up in a situation like this." That sounded pretty ironic coming from the guy who'd just escorted the victim's sister to the bedside. Well, not bedside yet.

She'd looked terrible sitting on a stiff couch in the ill-named "trauma family lounge." But when he'd tried again to comfort her while she waited for Max to come out of surgery, she'd barked at him to leave her alone. No matter what she said, Alex had no plans to leave until JJ's mother showed up. This didn't look like the kind of crisis anyone should face alone. He'd wait out an hour in this sad little cafeteria, then bring her some coffee and maybe try to get her to eat some breakfast.

"We're mixed up in it already. Really, Alex, I think you should go back to Denver."

There was a reason Alex called his brother Chicken Little when they were younger. The sky was always falling with Sam. And he usually wanted Alex to fix it. "They don't need me back at headquarters. A man's future is hanging in the balance here. I think *WWW* can handle any publicity woes."

He heard Sam pull a door shut and his brother's voice lowered to barely a whisper. "They're calling it equipment failure."

That sure sounded like studio types to him. "Come on, Sam, what did you think they were going to say? They can't very well stand up and boast that one of their production assistants dropped Max. Where was the guy on the belay line when Max fell, anyway?"

"The producer just roasted me in her office. She says the guy on the belay line is saying it was gear failure. Our equipment. They're saying it was *our* line and hardware that failed."

This was exactly why Alex had never been keen on this promotional venture in the first place. It raised their visibility, but it also made them a target for finger-pointing if anything went wrong. Adventure Gear didn't need the national exposure—they already had a good reputation among outdoor enthusiasts. The people who spent serious money on their gear knew AG products were top-notch. Alex never saw the point in high visibility to the reality television audience—he guessed ninety percent of them were couch potatoes who'd never seen the inside of a tent and never planned to. "They're blowing smoke. You know it's usually human error, and our stuff is better than that. And they aren't even using our SpiderSilk lines until next season."

"Not entirely."

The tiny red alarm in the back of Alex's mind that had started flashing hours ago suddenly bloomed into a full-blown wail. A surge of dread filled him so quickly he nearly lost the horrid coffee he'd just downed. *Oh, no.* The SpiderSilk prototype lines he'd delivered. They wouldn't, would they? Alex stood up, not caring that he knocked the chair back to rattle on the floor in the empty cafeteria. "Sam. Sam, tell me you did not allow *WWW* to use the SpiderSilk. They were only supposed to look at it for next season—not use it now. Tell me they weren't using the SpiderSilk. Tell me that right now."

The silence hit him like a brick wall.

"Right here, *right now,* Sam. Tell me you

didn't give them some kind of permission to use the SpiderSilk. Tell me Max Jones didn't fall from a rigging of the SpiderSilk."

"You'd said they were through testing."

Alex sank back to the table, stunned. *Oh, Father God, what have I done by stepping back and letting Sam run things? I knew something like this would happen if I left. I knew it and ignored it because I was sick of Sam.*

"I said they were through *initial* testing. That doesn't mean we're ready for a man to dangle from them. At night. In the rain. That's a brand-new coating we were using. What were you thinking?"

"You said it was like nothing we'd ever made before. We tested them way beyond fourteen kilonewtons. You said they would revolutionize the industry."

"*Next year.* When the UIAA approved them as *ready.* We tested for weight with traditional belay devices—not for rain or melting point.... They're *not* ready." Alex raked one hand through his hair, panic rising up his spine until it gripped his throat. "Sam, how could you do this? Do you have any idea what you've done? To Max? To us?"

"They were making noises like they'd go with someone else next season if we didn't sweeten the deal. They didn't want to wait until next year to showcase the SpiderSilk. They thought the unknown, the 'test pilot' element gave a great new twist. Hey, come on, the guy even knew he was using a prototype and signed a special release waiver and everything. And nobody said anything about a climb in the dark during bad weather."

"And it never occurred to you to ask me if I thought the SpiderSilk was ready?" Alex was shouting into his phone.

"Hey, you're the one who went AWOL and left me to run the company, remember?"

They'd had a million arguments like this in the past year. AG was second in market share, and Sam was gunning full out for the top spot. He'd always been a little too eager to cut corners in the name of flash and speed, and Alex had always been the one to stop him. In truth, at times Alex had been too cautious, and Sam's bold strokes had leaped the company forward to new heights. It was only recently Sam had begun to gamble on things that should never be risked. They'd fought so much in the past month that work had become torture. Alex had finally grown so weary of the constant battle that he had indeed taken a break to try to figure out if it was time to leave Adventure Gear altogether. It was the whole reason behind his seclusion in Gordon Falls—which was a joke, he realized. If he'd really wanted to get away, what was he doing secluding himself so close to where the show was?

"You should never have done that. Never."

"Well, I didn't think you much cared what I did anymore. They way you talked, you weren't coming back. Are you still walking away?"

A part of Alex—the squabbling sibling, angry, finger-pointing part—yearned to throw his hands up and do just that. In his two-week absence, Sam had managed to trash the Adventure Gear reputation it had taken Alex years to build. He wanted to say that he was done trying to rein Sam in, trying to hold on to integrity in a profit-hungry world. In this moment, Alex felt more than ready to leave AG in the dust and go get his joy back in some new adventure.

"I don't know." It was a truthful answer.

"We don't have the luxury of 'I don't know.' Fine, Alex, go ahead and disappear like you always do."

And that was just it. Alex did disappear. Too much. He'd come to realize that his "adventures" this past year were really just running away from the unpleasantness AG had become. Some part of Alex knew it was time to decide to either truly leave or truly stay. Nothing could have forced the issue more completely than the disaster that now lay in front of him. He wanted to have some comeback for the deserved accusation Sam just hurled at him, but he didn't have one.

Sam nearly growled into the phone, "Just know that this time I can't guarantee there will be an AG to come back to if you bolt again. At least I can say that I was doing what I thought was right for the company. Risks don't always pay off, and this one blew up in my face, but…"

"No, this one blew up in Max Jones's spine. A *man's life,* Sam."

"This is my doing—I get that."

"Do you? Do you really?" Alex wanted to think that Sam had finally made such a mess that he would wise up. A failed product or a botched marketing ploy was easy to shake off—for Sam, anyway. Had the cost finally been high enough to get through to Sam? Could he walk away and know Sam would pay attention to these kinds of issues in the future?

His brother's growl dissolved to a sigh. "We've been in worse scrapes than this, you know we have, and solving this kind of stuff is what you do best. Come on, Alex, you're our fix-it guy. You come up with the hot new product and then convince the world that they can't live without it. You can get the family on board with seeing things our way—I know you can. I'm asking you to help. But I'm not going to beg."

This wasn't a business decision anymore. JJ was upstairs wondering if her brother would ever walk again. For whatever reason, God had orchestrated him right into the middle of this storm, and he now knew he couldn't walk away from it. There would be no bolting—not even back to Denver.

"I'll stay here at the hospital until we get word on Max Jones. Get the ropes and hardware back from production and get Doc out here on the next flight." If anyone would be able to ascertain what had happened with the equipment, Mario "Doc" Dovini would. As their chief climbing expert and product development specialist in Denver, Doc would be the man with the answers. After all, they'd taken to calling the flamboyant Italian "Doc" because his diagnostic skills were so extraordinary.

"I got part of the gear back thirty minutes ago and Doc is due in at 10:48."

Maybe Sam was ready to take Adventure Gear's helm without him, after all. He had to be absolutely certain, though, and right now he was anything but sure.

He looked like a dead man.

That was all JJ could think of as she stared at the body on the bed in front of her. Enclosed in braces and packs and tubes and monitors, Max actually looked more like a machine than her brother. He was so banged up and trussed up that the only thing that still looked like Max was the hand lying beside hers on the stark white blanket. She put her hand on top of it, startled by how cold it was. She wanted the fingers to squeeze hers, to show some sign of life, but they were limp and still.

A nurse came up behind her. "They've made it so he can't move. He's in there, I promise you, but he'll be heavily sedated for a little while longer."

JJ looked back at the nurse. Hers was the first calm face JJ had seen in hours. "How bad is it?"

"He was one of the lucky ones. He made it here under the eight-hour window, which means they can give him drugs that improve his chances considerably. He had good care on site and they got him here fast."

"Max always said he wanted to ride in a

helicopter." She couldn't believe she was making a joke while her brother lay dying.

No, Max wasn't dying. At least now they were able to tell her that much. He'd definitely survive, only survival was going to be very different for a while. Maybe forever. JJ felt her throat tighten.

"Our boy has some fight in him, does he?" The nurse had a gentle smile.

"Loads."

Placing her hand on JJ's shoulder, the nurse gave her a quick squeeze. "That's good. He has excellent chances—you need to believe that. And those bruises will get worse before they get better, so he won't be winning any beauty contests anytime soon, but the tricky part's over for now." She nodded toward a vinyl couch against the windows. "That folds out if you want to try to nap—I'd guess you've been up for hours. I'm Leslie and I'll be on duty all today. What's your name, dear?"

"JJ. Max is my brother." JJ swiped a tear away with the back of her hand.

"It a comfort to have family here. Max is in expert hands—we're very good at what we do. We'll give him every chance there is, JJ, so you hang on to that." She punched a few buttons on one of Max's monitors. "What's JJ stand for?"

"Josephine Jones. It's always been a bit of a mouthful, so I've been JJ since I was about twelve."

Leslie ran an assessing hand along several of the way-too-many tubes traveling between Max and the assortment of machines that clustered around his bedside. "It's a good, strong name. Can I give you some advice, JJ?"

"I suppose."

"See all these machines? They're taking every burden we can off Max's body so that it can spend all its energy on healing. They look invasive, but they're really making things easier for Max. You should do the same. You and your family have a long road ahead of you, so it's time to pull in your own support. Call in your friends and Max's friends, and when they offer to help, don't think of them as invasive. Think of them as taking the burden off you so you can spend your energy on helping Max."

Sweet thoughts, but they sounded a bit rehearsed to JJ. "Do you say that to all the families?" It came out sharper than JJ would have liked, but she didn't really have a lot of grace to extend to anyone at the moment.

There was no judgment in Leslie's expression. "Just the ones who aren't crying."

"Not crying?"

"The ones who don't cry are the ones who are used to staying strong. Strong is a good thing—Max will need your strength—but this is one of those times where you'd better call in the cavalry. That's harder for some people than others. Just promise me that when people offer to help, you'll say yes."

"Call for backup." She was familiar with the concept. And yes, she'd always had a bit of trouble calling for backup before. Hadn't she just rebuffed Alex's multiple offers to help? It made JJ wonder if all ICU nurses had Leslie's high level of intuition.

Leslie smiled. "Exactly. Promise me you'll call for backup. And that includes me. I happen to know the coffee from the machine on the fourth floor is the only stuff in the hospital worth drinking." A nursing assistant knocked gently and then slid the glass ICU door open to reveal a cart full of bandages and such. "Stan and I have some less than dignified tasks to do to your brother. Why don't you take this chance to go get yourself some breakfast and make some calls? Max is out cold for the time being, and he'll want you here, on top of your game, later."

Whereas a few minutes ago the room felt small and claustrophobic like the inside of a combat vehicle, it suddenly felt wrong to leave Max. Her presence had turned into some kind of vigil to her, as if she were keeping Max alive—just one more responsibility she was taking on for his sake. How quickly she had catapulted herself back into big-sister mode, absorbing Max's self-inflicted catastrophes as some sort of failure on her part to keep him in line.

Leslie caught her hesitation. "Thirty minutes. It will do you good. Believe me, he's not going anywhere and he's very stable. Go on."

"Okay." JJ had to mentally command her feet to walk toward the door. Her head knew Leslie's advice was sound; it was her heart that wouldn't swallow the truth.

The glass doors closed behind her with an antiseptic swish, and JJ blinked in the stark light from the hallway windows. When had the sun come up?

Again, she forced her feet to move. It felt like her shoes echoed too loudly against the tiled floor and calm-colored walls until she pushed open the double doors that led out of the ICU unit. There, on the square navy couches she'd already come to hate, sat Alex. He looked like she felt, but he raised one of the two cups of coffee he held. "It's awful, but I thought you could use some."

Intrusive, but offering help. JJ could practically feel Leslie pushing her along toward the sad paper cup and its lukewarm contents. "Sure."

Chapter Four

They drank the horrid stuff in silence. Alex had a million things to say, but all of it seemed so trivial in the face of the circumstances. They had sat in silence several times together out on the dock, but it had felt much different. That silence had been warm and soft and effortless. This silence was cold and sharp, and holding it up was exhausting. Finally, just to break the quiet, Alex said, "I'm so sorry."

"Yeah," she muttered. The weariness in her voice was worse than the silence.

"I want to help, but I don't know how. Can you think of anything you need?"

JJ put down the cup and squinted her eyes shut. "I need Max to be okay."

Ouch. He'd been able to get word that Max had stabilized, pressing his position at Adventure Gear into a scrap of information from a nurse at the desk. She'd refused to tell him anything else and had insisted he shouldn't ask again. "He will." Of course, Alex had no basis whatsoever for the pronouncement, but it seemed downright cruel to say anything else.

"They're telling me he'll definitely live. It's more of a how question at the moment." JJ's eyes shot open, fire blazing behind the turquoise currently leveled straight at him. "It *is* a how question. Like how did this happen? Max knew how to climb. How did he fall?"

She stopped just short of saying, "Whose fault is this?" He answered it for her as carefully as he could.

"I don't know all the facts yet. People are scurrying all over the set trying to find things out, and I'm hearing conflicting reports." That wasn't exactly true, but Alex also knew that the only thing worse than no information was the wrong information. "It could've been a safety issue with the climbing site. Or the rain. Or bad knots or someone doing something they weren't supposed to, or all four. People tend to get stupid when the cameras start rolling. And not just the contestants."

She leaned against the couch's padded arm. "Max always had a gift for stupid ideas, especially with an audience."

Alex was sure *WWW* feasted on guys like Max. "Took all the double-dog dares as a kid?"

"Every one. Mom used to say he stayed up nights looking for ways to hurt himself." Her voice caught on the last two words.

Alex knew the type. Specializing in extreme gear as they did, those types were a big part of AG's customer base. Sam was one and had made a career out of knowing just how to push thrill seekers' buttons.

"I'm trying to find out what I can, but *WWW* isn't really sharing lots of information with us right now. Even though we're a major vendor, I don't have as much clout as you'd think. It may be you learn things before I do, seeing as your Max's family."

"Why isn't someone from *WWW* here?"

"There's someone on the way." He'd met the guy they were sending and had taken an instant dislike to him. Way too smooth. "You probably won't like him much."

"I skipped straight to hating *WWW* an hour ago when they wheeled Max out of surgery." She looked at him. "Why are you still here? Don't you have to go cover your corporate tail or something? Get legal on the phone?"

Alex didn't really know why he was still here. Did people think his leaving was just ditching blame, "covering his tail"? Her eyes told him that was exactly what people thought, and he couldn't refute it, could he? He did have a bad habit of ditching tough situations, and something told him that had to stop. It struck him that if he didn't stay—here, now—he never would. "I didn't think it was fair to leave you alone in all this."

That remark shot something through her spine. She sat up, defensive and prickly. "I'm a combat fire specialist. Army. I'm not some little girl whose hand you have to hold."

Funny, he'd wanted to do just that, take her hand, out on the dock or even in the helicopter when she'd let her head fall against the glass. "I know you can hold your own. I just don't want you to *have* to."

"I have friends." Defiance honed a sharp edge to her voice. She'd told him just the opposite out there on the docks—said that other than her brother and one cousin she didn't know people in Illinois and she rather liked it that way. He didn't doubt that she had friends who would love to be there for her, but the simple truth was she didn't have friends *nearby,* which made all the difference in a situation like this. Still, he was sure she'd never admit that.

"Okay." Alex drank his awful coffee and

stared at the industrial carpeting. They both sat in silence for a minute, then she let out a sigh that seemed to ease some of the iron from her spine.

"I didn't mean to snap at you." She pulled the elastic from her hair and then began nervously working it into a quick braid down her back. Efficient and out of the way. "That wasn't fair."

"None of this is fair. This is wrong in a million different ways, JJ. I'm so sorry."

"Yeah, well..." She waved off the rest of her sentence. Really, what was there to say?

Give me some kind words, Lord, Alex prayed, stretching his brain for something meaningful—and only coming up with lame platitudes and more apologies.

"Alex?"

Alex looked up to see a familiar face in an excruciatingly geeky turtleneck and cargo pants standing in the lounge doorway. Great. The only thing worse than *WWW*'s slick executive guy was the eccentric lawyer Sam had hired last year.

"Morning." The guy checked his phone, which was of course this year's latest gadget must-have. He looked at JJ and introduced himself. "Barry Morgan. AG legal."

JJ rolled her eyes and stood up. "Well, that didn't take long."

Barry had the nerve to look annoyed. "Sorry if I'm intruding, Miss…"

"I doubt that," JJ snapped back, then disappeared through the ICU doors, leaving behind the coffee and the muffins Alex hadn't even had a chance to offer without a second look.

"Nice going, Morgan." Alex didn't bother to hide his irritation. "That was Josephine Jones, Max Jones's sister. Was showing up here, now, really necessary?"

"I was in town giving a first pass at some sponsorship documents, so Sam begged me to come by and make sure we're on the same page. Sam would've come himself but he's going back to Denver tomorrow morning since you don't seem to want to leave. Chill out. I'm just here to talk to you—I'm not going to bother her."

"You just did. What can't possibly wait until Jones is awake and we know his prognosis?

"Hey, look, you should be glad I was nearby. *WWW*'s got guys all over this screaming we're liable. Already."

Alex pinched the bridge of his nose. "Of course they are." He gave Morgan his most direct look. "We are, aren't we?" He didn't even want to be having this conversation.

"Depends on your interpretation."

A very lawyerly answer from a guy who looked more like he belonged at a coffee bar than the American Bar Association. Where did Sam find these guys? "I'm sure." Alex waited for Morgan to snap open his leather messenger bag and hand over a stack of releases for JJ to sign, but the man simply sat down. "And what's your interpretation?" Alex prompted.

Morgan adjusted his artsy wire glasses. "The equipment we gave *WWW* was a prototype and not yet fully drop tested, right?"

"Not *we*. I never approved that. I only agreed to let them examine it—not use it. You should know that right now."

"Sam brought me up to speed on your opinion." He lowered his voice. "Look, the bottom line is that it'd be best for all concerned if we kept things as far from antagonistic with the victim and his family as possible. Sam's ticked you're not going to Denver, but I told him that you sticking around could be an advantage. I trust you're on board with that strategy?"

Alex didn't like people who used phrases like "on board" and "up to speed," especially while dressed like coffeehouse poets. "If you're asking me if I'm in favor of AG being in position to do the right thing here, then yes, I'm 'on board.'"

"Good. Your role is to stay in the family's good graces. If any suits are going to be filed, life will be far easier for us if they're directed at *WWW* and not AG. Surely you can see that."

The awful coffee in Alex's stomach turned more sour. "Oh, I can see exactly where you're heading with this."

"Excellent."

Alex stood. "And believe me, if you aren't out of this hospital within ten minutes you'll see just how 'up to speed' I can be, Morgan. If you think I'm here to cozy up to Jones's family for leverage..." Without finishing the vile thought, Alex picked up Morgan's bag and slapped it into the attorney's chest. "I'm here because a man's future is hanging in the balance, not because the profit share is in jeopardy. Leave. Now. And if you want anything, go call my brother. He speaks your language much better than I do."

This was exactly the kind of company Alex didn't want to run. Morgan was precisely the kind of person Alex never wanted to do business with. Was this the future of AG, or was there still time to turn things around?

That frustration, and the sleep deprivation, got the best of Alex because out of nowhere he shouted, "And for crying out loud, Morgan, does Sam know you do business looking like that?"

He was still there. Six hours had passed. JJ had walked out of ICU three times for food or phone calls about Mom's plane arrival or just to stop hearing the awful noise of those machines, and each time Alex Cushman was still camped out on the navy couch. After the second encounter, he'd simply stopped trying to make her talk to him. It was like Alex was keeping a silent vigil of his own. She didn't know what to do with that.

Suddenly feeling the exhaustion of the past twelve hours, JJ slumped down on the opposite couch. Alex held her gaze for a moment, looking as drawn as she felt. "I want to be furious with you, but I can't manage to pull it off."

One corner of his mouth turned up in a weak grin. "My irresistible charm?"

"More like I'm still awake and you're still here."

"So you'll begin despising me once you get a good night's sleep underneath you?"

His remark pricked a nerve. The raw nerve

that was stretched to breaking at the prospect of how long and how far it was from "here" to "okay." And that's if Max ever got to be "okay" ever again, which no one would tell her yet. If she heard the phrase "it's still too early to tell" one more time, she thought she'd scream. "I don't know when I'll get a good night's sleep ever again." JJ thought she was going to cry. She could feel the tight threat of tears grab hold of her throat, but then there was nothing. Empty. Dry. She'd spent months in the Afghan desert, fought fires in temperatures over 110 degrees, and she'd never felt this dry.

She'd come home hoping for a fresh start—a chance to find her feet again, find her purpose. Instead, she'd just found another disaster she could do next to nothing to fix.

Alex shook his head. "I'm so, so sorry."

There it was again, that awful silence where, in a less drastic situation, the other person was supposed to say, "It's all right." Only that didn't apply here. It was never going to be all right, not for Max. Today felt like the antithetical negative of the greeting-card phrase, "Today is the first day of the rest of your life." It was, but in all the horrible ways JJ could imagine. And she, who put out fires, who squelched disasters, couldn't do anything about it.

A doctor—one JJ recognized from the dozens who had slipped in and out of Max's room—pushed open the double doors that led into the lounge. He held one of those oversize manila envelopes that contained X-rays. "Miss Jones?"

She hated the look on his face. She knew that emotional mask, that "game face" for delivering news. She'd used it herself when she stood beside Captain Dewey to tell the brigade that Carlisle hadn't made it. A dreaded, familiar core of ice started in her gut and worked its way up to turn her chest cold and brittle. "Yes?"

JJ stood up, bracing herself.

He laid the envelope on the sticky coffee table and held out a hand. "I'm Dr. Ryland. We met a couple of hours ago, but I don't expect you to remember that. Does Max have other family on the way?"

"My mom is flying in. She'll be here around noon, I think."

"We're sending a limo to pick her up from the airport and bring her straight here," Alex said from behind her. For a moment she'd forgotten he was even in the room.

Dr. Ryland crossed his arms in front of his chest. "Leslie tells me you're a first responder."

"Army firefighter. Well, until last month, that

is. I finished my last tour of duty in Afghanistan recently."

"I've got some information on your brother's condition. Would you like it now or would you prefer to wait for your family? Normally I wouldn't offer a choice, but for someone with your background..."

With your experience handling disaster... JJ's brain finished the thought he hadn't.

"I should go." Alex's voice was soft, but it still startled her. Shouldn't he want to stay, get the latest report so he could update that annoying lawyer guy from before?

"Are you a friend of the family?" Dr. Ryland asked, clearly thinking JJ ought not to be alone with whatever news he was about to deliver.

"Well..." Alex stammered.

"It's complicated," JJ surprised herself by offering.

"It's your call." Dr. Ryland picked up the envelope. "Until Max is fully awake, you're making the decisions." His gaze passed back and forth between JJ and Alex. "A second set of ears is a good thing, but you can wait until your family is here."

JJ stared at the envelope. It held Max's future. How on earth could she wait? But did she really want to handle it alone?

"I should go," Alex repeated.

"No." It was like the words were coming out of someone else's mouth. "No, stay."

Dr. Ryland looked at both of them again as he flicked on the white light box that would hold the X-ray. "You're sure?"

"No," said JJ, "but that's the best I can do for now."

They stood in the bleary pale light of the box while Dr. Ryland clipped three different X-rays onto the display. JJ sucked in a lungful of air, and she felt Alex's hand steady her shoulder from behind. She'd never seen a fractured spine before, but it didn't take a medical degree to see the damage. The terms and phrases coming from the doctor blew over her like gale winds, hard and relentless. She heard them but didn't register them. She nodded once or twice, heard Alex ask a question, but the room was closing in on itself until a single word snapped everything into focus: *Unlikely.*

"It's unlikely Max will regain use of his legs. I won't say never because I've seen enough surprises in my day and Max was in excellent physical shape."

JJ hated that he'd used the past tense. Something hot and white and unreasonable started boiling in her stomach. She clenched her fists, forcing the air in and out of her lungs.

"His hands and fingers may regain a good deal of functionality with therapy. The position of the..." More medical jargon, more terms and percentages and cautious language. JJ held up a hand to stop the spew before it swallowed her.

"Max will never walk again." She looked straight into Dr. Ryland's eyes, daring him to take back the awful truth behind his careful words.

"It's unlikely. Not with these injuries. But I want you to remember that he is alive and he will recover."

"Recover? Recover what?"

"Every single bit of function we can preserve for him. We are the leaders in this field, Miss Jones. Max will have therapies and treatments that are cutting edge, and even experimental ones if he chooses." Dr. Ryland stared hard into JJ's eyes. "His life is not over, no matter how it seems to you right now. And when he wakes up, he'll need to see you believe in him and his future. Max is alive. Don't ever forget that."

"But he can't walk. Ever." The thing building inside her, the pent-up fear and anger, refused to be contained. "Ever again."

"The doctor didn't say that," Alex's voice was disgustingly reasonable. Condescending, even.

"You don't belong here," JJ blurted out, the white-hot thing boiling up beyond her control. "You did this to Max. He's here because of you."

Dr. Ryland put a hand on her shoulder. "Miss Jones…"

"Don't!" JJ snapped her head around, livid at how calm they both were. She focused her glare on Alex. "Leave. Now. I hope I never see you again."

Chapter Five

JJ watched her mother a few hours later as Dr. Ryland went through the same jumble of cautionary language he had with her. It was hard, watching the emotions she knew so well play out on her face. Max had been a tornado of trouble from the day he started walking. Mom and Dad had been awakened by police and done the dash to the ER with a bloodied Max more times than she could count, but everyone knew this was different. Max wasn't coming back from this the same way. JJ tried to be grateful Max was coming back at all, but she wasn't so good at that right now.

"He's extraordinarily fortunate," Dr. Ryland said. He looked like he meant it, but again, it was impossible to grasp the silver lining in any of this. She couldn't help but read her own thoughts—*he's lucky to be alive at all*—into his pronouncement. "He had good care and quickly. Those things matter a great deal in cases like this. For the injury he has, I'm optimistic about his prospects."

Optimistic. How many times had JJ heard that word in the last day? She'd grown to hate it in all its careful use.

Dr. Ryland steepled his hands on his desk as if he had something important to say. Out of the corner of her eye, JJ caught Mom clutching her handbag. "Max will be alert enough to begin asking questions soon, so I'd like to discuss how we share his diagnosis with him. As you can imagine, this can be a difficult task. His body has been through a lot of trauma, and based on what you all have told me about his personality, I think it's smart to assume that he won't take the news well."

"Who could ever take news like this well?" JJ caught a hefty dose of panic in her mother's voice.

"Believe it or not, we're actually glad when they get angry," Dr. Ryland assured. "Anger means he's invested in getting past this—that he hasn't given up. It takes a fair amount of fight to come back from something like this. I know it will be uncomfortable for you, but if Max gets emotional and belligerent, I'd take that as a good sign."

"Max pitches a great fit," JJ replied, just picturing the tirade Max would likely throw. She'd seen him fly off the handle for far less. "If fight is a good sign, then Max is in great shape." She filled her voice with enthusiasm she didn't feel.

"This is hardly the time for cracks like that." Her mother's scowl was brittle and terse. It reminded JJ of her father and his military distaste for weakness of any kind.

They hadn't really gotten along in the years before he died, despite JJ joining the army. Dad had lived and breathed military service in a way that JJ never could. His home had been his own personal battleground, run with absolute authority. No insubordination or weakness allowed.

Once she'd enlisted, JJ had hoped Dad would view her as more of an equal. When she'd come home on leave, shaken by what she'd seen, she'd tried to confide in him—to share her questions and anxieties. The conversation had been an absolute disaster. He couldn't understand how battle had affected her in ways so different than his own experiences. When she'd tried to express doubts about what she saw, he would never hear it. He died three years ago while she was still on duty, yet from his grave she still felt his disappointment in her weak and troubled homecoming. JJ couldn't shake the feeling that Arnie Jones was now fully disappointed in both his children.

"Actually, it is a perfect time for jokes." Dr. Ryland leaned in, taking off the thick horn-rimmed glasses that gave him such an authoritative air. "Humor is one of our best weapons in this. As are calm and strength. Which is why, Mrs. Jones, I'd recommend that JJ and I be the ones to tell him."

"Why?" Her tone provided the most convincing argument for Ryland's strategy, sad and full of a mother's worry.

"No mother on Earth could deliver such news without tremendous emotion. I'd only ask you to do so if we had no other options. He can't yet respond to you while the breathing tube is in place, so it's a delicate balance to let him respond fully without the ability to speak. It can be hard."

When JJ's mother balked, the doctor held up a hand. "Of course, you are welcome to do whatever you choose—the decision is entirely up to you—but I thought you would want to consider my suggestion. JJ's had a little bit more time to come to grips with the whole situation and her background gives her more experience with these sorts of situations." He paused to let the point sink in, then moved on from delivery to content.

"Now is not the time for cold hard facts. It would be best if we could lead Max up to his diagnosis in bits, not all at once. I do admit there isn't much hope for Max to walk, but I don't think it's wise to take all of that hope away right now. The last thing we want is for Max to give up. We need him fighting."

"I'll do it." JJ had tried not to ask this question, but now it couldn't be helped. "Is he...all there? Brain-wise?" The words felt ugly and cumbersome, and she hated the resulting panic on her mother's face.

"Cognitively, we've every reason to believe Max is fine. He's on a lot of medications, so he isn't quite himself, but we don't see any evidence of brain damage." Dr. Ryland gave her mother a gentle look. "If it helps, he'll probably have no memory of the accident. He might not even remember today or tomorrow, so JJ, this likely isn't a conversation you'll have only one time. I like to think that takes a bit of the pressure off this first time. You will need to talk to him again once his breathing tube is out and he's more able to respond."

JJ shrugged. "I wish that helped, but it doesn't." How do you tell someone you love that their life has changed forever? That they are broken in ways that can never be fixed? How do you say that not just once, but over and over again, seeing them react to it with fresh hurt each time? Thoughts tumbled over one another in her head. She felt alone in the room, isolated as if she were back standing in the middle of the Afghan desert with a sandstorm swirling around her.

She tried to mentally reach for something calming—a time and a place when she felt centered and relaxed. The first memory that came to mind was sitting on the dock with Alex. Scowling, she pushed the thought away. Memories of the friendship she'd thought she'd found were *not* going to help her now.

This felt so far out of her depth that JJ was sure ten hours of pondering wouldn't prepare her to tell Max what she needed to tell him—and according to Dr. Ryland, she had an hour.

She stood up. "All right, Dr. Ryland, I'll be the one to tell him with you. But I have no idea how to do it."

* * *

"You? You hurt my boy?" Mrs. Jones's anguish was so heartbreaking Alex was regretting introducing himself in the hospital hallway.

"My company is one of the vendors to the show where Max was hurt." It was a correction he was sure the woman didn't hear.

She clutched her handbag and glared at him. "You let Max do this to himself. For television. And now look what's happened! Arnie would run you over with a tank for what you've done to our son."

He said the only thing that might help. "I'm so very sorry for what's happened to Max. Please believe I'm trying to arrange for every possible assistance and to make sure he gets the best of care. If there's anything you need…"

"I need my son to get better." Her words were sharp and filled with anger. JJ looked so much like her mother that Alex felt the sting that much more. "Can you make that happen, Mr. Cushman? Can you?"

She walked away, leaving Alex to slump against the walls and pray for some way to fix the unfixable. He could live a hundred years and still remember that look, surely. A mother's agony—was there anything more heartbreaking? She wasn't handling things well, he could tell. Then again, who could handle something like this well? There was pain everywhere Alex looked, with more than enough blame and resentment to go around and nowhere near enough hope.

No wonder he went looking for the hospital chapel.

It was a small room, soft and quiet with muted lighting and lots of wood. A stained glass window depicting a waterfall sent blues and greens into one corner of the room. Not more than twelve padded pews faced a simple cross set atop a draped table. Every pew held a box of tissues. This wasn't a room for happy ceremonies; this was a place of grief and solace.

He recognized the blond braid in the third pew immediately and almost turned and left the room. It was her sniffle, the small shake of her shoulders, that pulled his hand from the door handle. Her silhouette was completely different from the last time he'd seen her; she appeared deflated rather than defiant. JJ was hanging on by a thread if she was hanging on at all. No one should have to do that alone.

"JJ?"

Her head whipped around and her shoulders snapped straight as if she were embarrassed to be found there. The fire was there in her eyes, but they were the red-rimmed eyes of someone who'd just cried, and cried hard. She gave him a "You again?" glare but said nothing.

"I didn't come looking for you. I came looking for God, actually, so this seemed a good place to start." He really hadn't expected to find her in here. He waited for her to yell at him to leave. When she didn't, he took another step toward her. "Are you…are you all right?" It was a dumb question—anyone could see she was miles from "all right." He hadn't seen her in the past few hours. She looked like she'd been through a war in that time. "Did something happen?"

She glanced upward, pulling in a breath to right another wave of tears. "I just told him."

"Told him?"

A tear made its way down her cheek. She had these kid-like freckles that didn't seem to belong on such strong features. "I just told Max his legs no longer work. Dr. Ryland and I told him together. For the first time. It was awful. He cried. I mean, not out loud—he can't with the breathing tube and all—but I could still see it. It was all over his face, the pain in his eyes and the tears on his cheeks."

"That must have been terrible." It seemed

so inadequate a thing to say, but every other phrase that came to mind felt just as useless. "I'm sure he was glad to have you beside him, to be the one to give him the news. That's unbelievably brave, JJ. Really."

"Dr. Ryland thought I'd be the best one to be there. He picked right up on Mom's panic and knew Max needed calm. Seems like a smart guy."

"He's the best. Top five in the country, they tell me."

That sent more tears down JJ's face. "He doesn't even look like Max right now, with his face all swollen and those bruises. I can't even say for sure he understood what I told him. The doctor says his memory is a bit sketchy right now so he won't really remember." She balled a tissue up in her fist. "I'll have to tell him over again. Maybe even a couple of times. I hate this. All this mindless coping, this sitting around waiting for tests or medicines or symptoms or whatever… It feels rotten. I need to do something."

Alex sat down on the pew next to her. "I think you just did something. Something huge."

JJ pulled the elastic out of her braid and began unraveling it with her fingers. "You know, I probably should have yelled at him.

Dressed him down for the stupid risks he's always taking. You can never get a word in when you argue with Max, and this was my one chance where he couldn't yell back. Only… only…" Her voice fell off and she reached for another tissue.

Only. If only. The words were pounding in his own head like a migraine.

"Why aren't you gone?" The words held none of her earlier anger, but more of a weary befuddlement.

"I'll go when you tell me I should."

She rolled her eyes. "I already told you to leave."

"Yeah, that one didn't really count."

She blinked at him, both eyebrows arched. "Because…"

"You know, I don't really know. Something just told me you shouldn't be alone yet."

"My mom is here."

"Oh, I know." Alex pinched the bridge of his nose. "Your mother just laid into me in the hallway. She actually told me your father would have run me over with a tank. You didn't tell me you came from a military family."

She gave a small laugh, tiny and thin but there nonetheless. "Went all 'if General Jones were here' on you, did she? It's a favorite tactic of hers, telling us what Dad would have done. Dad could be quite the dictator when he got mad. It's how she kept us in line as kids, telling us what kind of lecture we had to look forward to when he got back from his latest deployment and learned what we'd done." She sighed. "Still, I thought she saved that for offspring."

"She's worried and angry. I'm as good a target as any, I suppose."

The look on her face told him JJ had endured her share of dressing-downs at her father's hands. The exact opposite of his and Sam's dad, who could never scrounge up enough attention for his sons to get angry. Some shrink somewhere would surely draw a straight line from Sam's high-maintenance personality to their father's lack of family focus.

As for Alex, was it any surprise that he coped by putting distance between himself and his problems? He'd never been able to fix his family, and the harder he'd tried to hold them all together the more they'd fractured apart. Alex was a problem solver, all right, but he'd learned not to get too close or too invested in those problems. His best solutions came from the mile-high view—using distance to gain perspective. So why was he down in the thick of it now?

JJ shook her head. "I'm sorry."

Her words startled Alex. "Wait a minute—your brother's been injured by my equipment and your mom takes it out on me and *you're* apologizing? What's wrong with this picture?"

JJ's gaze snapped to him, her face going pale. "So you know for certain? It was a failure of your equipment?"

Alex wanted to punch himself in the nose. He hadn't meant to say that. No one really knew if that was true, at least not yet. Her unearned apology had shocked it out of him. Now there wasn't a way to back down from the admission, even though he was sure JJ and her family would jump on anything that didn't make this Max's fault. "We don't actually know yet. I shouldn't have said something like that." Even as he said the words, he knew they'd have no effect.

"But the show told us it was probably equipment failure. Your equipment? Is that why you're staying so close and being so friendly? You keep saying how badly you feel about the whole thing."

"JJ, it's just not that simple. SpiderSilk was an experimental product, yes, but it had been tested to thousands of pounds of force so we don't yet know what happened. My brother, Sam, approved the use because he believed he was giving *WWW* a solid prototype." The words tasted bitter and hollow in his mouth. It was Sam's style to offer up convenient half-truths, not his.

Her eyes narrowed. "You are the worst kind of liar."

She'd seen right through his doubts. "I'm telling you the truth."

"But not all of it." She stood up. "Really, I was hoping for better out of you. Or was all that on the dock just another sales job?"

Alex planted himself between JJ and the chapel door. "Hey, look, the truth—the *full* truth—is that I don't know enough yet to be able to tell you for certain. Sam was using SpiderSilk, and that's not a retail product yet. We didn't give it to the show to use. They were supposed to be examining it for the next season once we were a hundred percent sure it was market ready. But it has been tested extensively. It shouldn't have failed under the conditions *WWW* used it. We're not even sure the SpiderSilk is what failed. I can't give you a definitive explanation right now, even though I know you want one. But I'm not here because of that. I'm here because I want to help you. And part of that means giving you the most accurate facts I can.

Seems to me the last thing you need right now is wrong information."

"Oh, and you're an expert on what I need." She turned and picked up her sweater off the pew.

"I'm not claiming to be an expert. I'm just trying to do what I can. Your focus is exactly where it should be—on Max's treatment and his recovery process. Anything else can wait until we've had a chance to figure out exactly what happened." He sighed. "It's not as simple as bad ropes—we hadn't trained any of the techs at *WWW* on how to use SpiderSilk. They didn't have the recommended belay devices. They undid the rigging so we can't see what knots they used. So we honestly don't know whether it was a failure of SpiderSilk that caused Max's fall. At least not yet."

"I don't think Max much cares about that right now." Her eyes filled with hurt. "How long have you known it could have been the..." She waved her hands in the air, reaching for the brand name Alex had always found so unforgettable.

"SpiderSilk?"

"Yes. How long have you known he fell using that? Have you known *this whole time?*" Her tone on those last three words just about broke Alex's heart.

"I meant what I said—I don't know anything for certain yet. All I know is that my brother gave *WWW* permission to climb with Spider-Silk under certain conditions, complete with waivers that Max agreed to sign. But maybe I can know more soon. We managed to get some of the lines from *WWW* so we can examine them. Our technician got in yesterday and he's going over all the equipment—not just the SpiderSilk but everything Max was using when he fell."

JJ shoved one arm through the sleeve of her sweater. It was July, but the hospital seemed to house a sterile chill in every room. "You didn't answer my question. How long have you known?"

She glared at him, and Alex knew every aspect of how they treated each other from here on in would hinge on what he said next. "I've known it was a possibility since a little while after we got here."

Something shut in her eyes. Alex's skin prickled at the defensive posture that seemed to overtake her body. If a person could have inner armor, he'd just seen it lock down tight. Without a word—but with a message so clear it made a hollow hole in his chest—she left the room.

Chapter Six

"Wait, now?" Sam barked over the phone. "You're coming to Denver *now?*"

Alex handed his passport to the security officer. The thing was so bedraggled and covered in stamps it never ceased to cause stares.

"You know," Alex said as he tossed his bag onto the conveyor belt and began emptying his pockets into a plastic bin. "You might want to be thankful my plane's going to Denver and not Fiji. If you wanted to convince me I'm done with AG, you're coming really close to succeeding."

"We had a plan. We'd decided you were going to stay there. You were supposed to…" Alex didn't hear anything else as he jabbed the power button on his phone with an angry grunt and tossed it into the screening bin, too. They'd had a plan? Alex hadn't felt like they'd been running AG on the same plan for months. The team excitement, the rush of partnership—all that was gone. Picking his wallet and keys back up on the other side of the security screening, his eye caught the departure display above him listing a flight to Singapore. The urge to run surged up with a power that astonished him.

Just go. Leave it all behind. You've lost your way and you won't find it in Denver. Go far. Far.

Distance called to him like the antidote to everything that was too close and too tight. For one irrational second, Alex thought about "forgetting" his phone in the little plastic bin and just walking away from everything.

But Max couldn't walk away from anything now. This problem was too big to discard. And although it sounded wonderful, even Singapore's misted mountains wouldn't wipe the last look JJ had given him from his memory. No, that look burned at him every time he closed his eyes. He had promised to leave when she told him to go, and she had clearly told him to leave when she walked out of the chapel. It was better for everyone if he went back to the office in Denver and tried to see what could be done. He should have been glad to be getting out of ground zero for this disaster.

He wasn't. Not in the least.

Instead, Alex slumped into an AG van at the Denver airport hours later feeling twice as exhausted as when he took off. He might as well have never left Chicago because JJ followed him everywhere. On the plane, he'd encountered a hundred reminders of her. That scarf was the color of her eyes, this magazine article had her tone of voice, a pair of children down the aisle made him wonder what Max and JJ had been like as youngsters. Alex's gift for geographically stuffing miles between himself and problems had always worked—until now. Now the farther he ran, the closer she felt. It was making him nuts.

"Red Rocks."

"Sir?" The driver turned to look at him, stumped by the request to visit Denver's outdoor amphitheater.

"Take me to Red Rocks."

It bothered Alex that he didn't recognize the driver's face—there was a time he'd known every AG employee by name. Not all the sales staff in all the stores, of course, but everyone out here at the national office.

"I don't think there's anything going on there today," the driver said. "Don't you want to go see Mr. Cushman—I mean, the *other* Mr.

Cushman? Drop your bags at the office or your apartment or something?"

All of those places felt entirely too tight at the moment. Alex needed space. Sky. Sun. The spectacle of God's palette. He peered at the driver's name tag. "Rory?"

"Yes, Mr. Cushman?"

"I just need an hour at Red Rocks. Where do you like to eat?"

Rory, still baffled, rattled off two or three fast-food burger joints.

"Stop at the first one you see and I'll buy lunch for both of us. You'll get an hour's paid lunch while you wait for me at Red Rocks. Work for you?"

Rory looked like he'd just been asked to disobey orders.

"An hour, Rory. Then you can deliver me to AG like you've been told."

A guilty look flashed across the young man's face. "They said you were kind of crazy."

Kind of crazy? People used to call him a visionary. His passion for what AG did used to light up a room of sales managers. What was crazy was how things had spun out of control to the point they had. "Not today, just hungry."

Rory put the van in gear. "Whatever you say, Mr. Cushman."

* * *

The burger sat untouched on the top row of benches in the massive outdoor amphitheater. A few visitors joined Alex in the sweeping rows of benches, tourists snapping photos of the slabs of red rock that jutted into the sky and gave the theater its name. The occasional athlete ran up and down the steps—a killer workout Alex's knees could no longer manage. It was hot, but Alex welcomed the sensation after so much time in the cool sterile hospital and airport atmosphere. For whatever reason, Red Rocks had always been where he went to think. Just far enough from the office to feel "away," and just close enough to provide an easy escape. Sometimes he'd walk the rows of bench seats as if it were a labyrinth, considering problems as he mounted steps. He could always see a solution from the top, but today he just sat still, willing the space and light to bring him some kind of calm.

Where is my fault in this, Lord? What could I have done that would have Max Jones walking today? Is this the unavoidable fate of an AG that climbed too far too fast? He'd never been the kind of guy to feel guilty—sometimes even about things he ought to regret—and this wave of doubt and remorse had him reeling.

Every time he sat still waiting for answers, all he'd end up with was another pile of disturbing questions.

"Not hungry?"

Alex looked up, startled to hear the familiar Italian accent. "What are you doing here?" Doc was supposed to be doing equipment forensics in Illinois, not standing over him in Denver.

Doc sat down, immediately poking through the bag and pulling out a handful of French fries. "I brought the equipment here. Better tools, less nervous television people." He narrowed one eye. "But more Samuel." He bit into a fry. "Your brother is in a panic."

Alex picked up the drink he'd left untouched, suddenly thirsty. "When isn't Sam in a panic?"

"Ah, but this one, he deserves."

Doc's tone sent a shock of ice down Alex's spine despite the strong sun. "Meaning?"

Fishing in his pocket, Doc pulled out a sheet of paper and unfolded it onto the bench between them. "SpiderSilk is at fault. Not entirely at fault, but at fault just the same."

"Want to explain what that means?"

Doc leaned back on his elbows. "The situation was badly handled. SpiderSilk is much lighter and thinner than our other lines. The belay devices they used aren't what we would have specified, and the fact that it was nighttime and raining made things worse. If you ask me, they never should have attempted the rappel down the wall under those conditions with any line, much less an untested prototype. And your Mr. Jones was not taking the time a smart climber would under the circumstances. Those things turned a small problem with the fiber into a big one."

Alex's throat went dry. "The fiber..."

"We test for lots of things, but we had not yet started testing for lots of things together." Doc ran his hands down a series of equations Alex knew were tension test results, fiber composition diagrams and other such calculations. "As it turns out, the right combination of friction, moisture and carelessness can compromise this fiber if you put multiple surges of force on it."

"Like a daredevil contestant wanting to make a spectacular landing for the television cameras."

Doc nodded. "You know Samuel is not my favorite Cushman," he began, quoting an old joke between him and Alex, "but in his defense, what *WWW* did with the rigging isn't anything close to what they told your brother they would be doing. It was a risky but reasonable scenario the way they first described it. Had it been up to me, I still would have said no, but…"

"But Sam should have known you can't count on people like that to stick to plans. Wind, rain, night climb—all they could see was a riveting drama that would make great television. Of course the safer plan got thrown out when a more exciting opportunity presented itself. It was bound to happen. Why am I the only Cushman who could see that?"

"Because you are not Samuel. And Samuel is not you. Samuel finds the deal and makes the deal. You see the experience, the product, the person." Doc had a bad habit of waxing philosophical at the wrong moment. He always blamed it on his Italian blood, but Alex thought it more a product of personality than genealogy.

"I don't see much of anything right now but disaster."

Doc looked at him, his dark eyebrows furrowing in analysis. Alex was none too fond of having that scrutiny turned to him. "It is a disaster," Doc replied. "A man can no longer walk." He paused, clearly waiting for something from Alex.

"Yes." Alex agreed. "I know. That's why I came back to Denver to solve this."

"Ah, but *why* did you come back to Denver?

I expected to find you in Dubai this morning, not Denver. The Alexander I know would be halfway around the world by now."

"You need me here."

Doc was one of those people who could spot an evasion from a mile off. It was an infuriating trait, but his eye for minute detail was what made him such a great product development researcher. He said nothing, only popped another fry into his mouth while he produced what Alex and Sam had come to call "Doc's Eyes of Death."

Alex stood up and paced the aisle between the rows of seats. "Okay, I don't exactly know why I'm here. We've ruined a man's life, Doc. Max Jones will never walk again, his family is an angry army of grief and blame and there's nothing to be done for any of it. There's no way to make this right, ever."

"And you hate unsolvable problems. They are your favorite thing to run from—we all know that."

If Doc was referring to the all-night conversation they'd had the night before he left on his "sabbatical," Alex didn't appreciate the reference. He was right about one thing—his relationship with Sam had become an unsolvable problem and he did want to leave it behind.

Badly. "I know SpiderSilk was my baby, but this one is all Sam's fault. I'm so angry at him I don't know what I'll do when I see him—but it won't be productive, I'll tell you that. I don't want to be anywhere near him, but I don't trust him to do damage control. I don't trust him at all."

Doc polished off the last of Alex's fries without apology and crumpled the bag. "So you are here because you could run? Or because you couldn't?"

"I have no idea." Actually, he did. Only the burning glare of JJ Jones's eyes wasn't a reason. Not a sane one, anyway. She was like some kind of freakish magnet, a line tethering him to the disaster. "She blames me. Why does she blame me when she should blame Sam? Or her brother? Or *WWW?* Believe me, there's plenty of blame to go around."

"Jones's sister? The one you took to the hospital?"

"JJ. I can't get the way she looks at me out of my head. Like I just shot her in the stomach or something. I mean, I can't really blame her for being upset, and the fact that I was there made me an easy target, but it gets to me in a way that just makes everything worse. Nothing—*nothing*—would be helped by getting personally involved here. It's awful, what happened—I know that. But I think this may just be the thing that pulls AG under, and Doc, that scares the skin off me right now."

"But you've been threatening to leave for months. We all thought you were leaving before this, actually. I know your brother did. What is it to you if AG goes under?"

He said it so casually. As if the dismantling of ten years of work—not to mention the evaporation of his own job—was as easy as tossing out the garbage. "You don't mean that."

Doc sighed—an old man's sigh, reminding Alex that the Italian climber had a good twenty years on him. "Neither do you. I have always wondered what it would look like when you ran out of escape clauses. In this case, you have to turn around and stand your ground, and you don't have any idea how to do that, do you?"

"There may be no ground for AG to stand on."

Doc's eyes narrowed. "I wasn't talking about AG. I don't think you were, either. Aren't you smart enough to realize this isn't about AG? It's about you and Samuel. It's about this Miss Jones and her brother and what your fighting with Samuel has done to them." He shook his head. “Really, I am surprised you’re not at the North Pole.”

Alex didn’t have a response. He hated everything Doc was saying, detested the ring of truth the man’s words had. God had been after him for months to do something about his relationship with Sam, to get to the heart of why they fought the way they did and fix it, and Alex had refused. Stalled, excused, rationalized, whatever it took to sidestep the issue. Doc was right—this had become about so much more than faulty lines or shortcut prototypes. This was about the damage done by a partnership gone wrong and left to fester.

Alex let his head fall into his hands. “I know I need to hash this out with Sam—once and for all—but…not yet. I’m supposed to be in Illinois, Doc. I can’t shake it. Right now—” Alex peered up into his friend’s eyes “—I’m pretty sure staying with the problem means going back to Illinois. Does that make any sense?”

“Believe it or not, it does. And it doesn’t. But that is the kind of thing I expect from you.” He grabbed the crumpled bag. “I’ll drive you back to the airport.”

“Rory is here waiting.”

“No, he’s not. I sent him home when he called the office to say where you were. I had

Cynthia fetch me your Go-Bag before I drove out here. Believe it or not, I came out here to convince you to stay out of Samuel's way for now."

Alex's Go-Bag was a fully packed duffel with a week's worth of clothes that he kept in a closet in his office for times when he chose to disappear overnight. His assistant Cynthia was charged with keeping it ready at all times. It irked Alex to no end that Doc knew about it, knew to ask Cynthia and knew he'd turn around and go back to Chicago.

Alex Cushman was supposed to be less predictable than that.

Chapter Seven

JJ couldn't believe it when she walked down the hall to find Alex back at his perch on the tiresome blue couch. When someone mentioned to her that he'd left this morning, she'd told herself to be glad she was rid of this guy. Now he was back? Already? She crossed her arms and sat back on one hip. "Don't you ever go away?"

He looked up with surprisingly weary eyes. "I was heading back to Gordon Falls for the night and thought maybe you'd appreciate a lift. I can have the helicopter bring you back first thing in the morning. I'm sure you need a change of clothes, if nothing else."

That took a lot of nerve. He of all people knew he'd yanked her out of her cottage in the middle of the night and she hadn't been back since. Where did he get off taking some kind of backhanded pity on her rumpled appearance? JJ's cousin, Charlotte, who lived in Chicago, had sent keys to her tiny apartment while she was away on an importing trip, but it barely sufficed. All the shuttling back and forth to the hospital meant JJ could barely find ten minutes in a shower, much less a decent wardrobe change.

"It's a three-hour drive, JJ. You'd eat up half a day just getting there and back. I can have you in Gordon Falls in forty minutes. You could fix yourself dinner in your own kitchen. Sleep in your own bed. Think of it."

The craving to get out of here washed over her with startling force. Her eyes fell closed for a second, hungry for peaceful sounds of the river. Some actual food. The last piece of apple pie sitting uneaten in her fridge. A full breath of sweet riverbank air. One night out there would perk her up like a thousand cups of coffee. She needed it, and badly. Badly enough to consider taking Alex Cushman up on his disingenuous offer.

"Come on," he sighed, frustration twisting his voice. "I'm trying hard to be nice here."

That was it, wasn't it? "You're trying really hard. And I can't help but wonder why."

He ran his fingers though his sandy-blond

hair. "To be perfectly honest, I don't really know why."

Come to think of it, he didn't look much better than she did. They must really be panicked up there at *WWW* and Adventure Gear. After all, she didn't think he was supposed to divulge as much of what he knew as he had in the chapel.

He added, "I'm stumped, actually. I'm usually the first person out the door when complications like this happen."

"Is that what Max is to you?" she snapped back, annoyed at herself for even beginning to fall for his clever act. "A *complication?*"

"No. Not at all. That's just it…Max is a person. A man. Someone whose life is forever changed and I can't do anything to make it right again." He fisted his hands and looked at her. "Look, I don't know what I'm doing here. I don't know why I can't get your brother—or you—out of my head when putting things out of my mind is ordinarily a particular gift of mine."

He stood up and began pacing. "Not that I didn't try." He flipped one hand toward the window. "I couldn't even get as far as Denver, and normally I'd be in another hemisphere with something like this. Sticking around to beat my head against problems I can't fix isn't my style. And there's nothing I can really change here. I don't have the slightest idea what I'm doing, only that I can't..." He clamped his hands on either side of his face as if the notion actually gave him a headache. "I can't...not...help even though I don't see how I *can* help." His ventured another look at her with pained eyes.

She had to give Alex Cushman one thing—the man radiated charisma. His presence filled the room wherever he went. A quick Internet search the other night had told her Alex was the bold visionary behind Adventure Gear, the world-traveler enthusiast who embodied the company's high-energy, high-integrity reputation. Where Sam Cushman was the clever empire builder, Alex was the free-spirit driving force behind the brand.

True to his last comment, he also had earned a reputation for disappearing overnight, often at inopportune moments. According to the magazine profiles—and there were many—Alex got away with it because most of those times he showed up weeks later with some exotic new idea that became AG's next hot product.

To a small but enthusiastic audience, Alex was an icon. Even though she'd never heard of him, people seemed to follow him almost more than they followed Adventure Gear. He was Steve Jobs mixed with Indiana Jones with a bit of rock star folded in. The photos she saw portrayed a carefree explorer, a handsome treasure hunter living the life other people could only dream of. That man bore little resemblance to the disheveled guy grasping at words in front of her.

"I'm not trying to play you, JJ," he said so softly she could barely hear him. "Can you believe that?"

Six months ago she would have laughed at a speech like that and walked away. Afghanistan's first lesson had been that "allies" who insisted they were trustworthy were usually the first to fire once your back was turned. Now, drained and wound too tightly, enough of her—maybe too much of her—was eager to believe him. Nurse Leslie's words, not to mention the compelling intensity of Alex's eyes, kept chipping away at her resolve. When Max wasn't lashing out at everything and everyone, he was a wounded pile of grief. Mom was at a total loss for what to do and how to behave, waffling between giving orders and fits of tears.

All of which made a night out of here feel incredibly tempting. She really did need to swap out her clothes and put a few details in order—

she didn't have too many friends in Gordon Falls to call on for help just yet, so everything that needed to be done, she'd have to do herself. And then afterward...her own bed. Oh, the bliss a good night's sleep in her own bed would be. And he was right—she'd never get faster transportation to and from home than Alex's helicopter.

"I'll take you up on your offer. But, just to be clear, I don't know if I believe you." She felt compelled to add, "Yet." She held his eyes, giving him her best combat "don't mess with me" glare.

"Fair enough." Alex took out his cell phone and began punching in numbers. "I'll meet you downstairs in the lobby in twenty minutes."

This felt wrong. That was the only thought pounding through Alex's head as he found himself out on the Gordon Falls river dock again in the middle of the night. Alex's talent was usually his ability to find peace in the craziest of settings, to dig out the nugget of adventure waiting underneath every pile of chaos. The more chaos, the more he became energized by the prospect of a rich adventure to take him away from it all. And then he'd come back with a solution. That was how it always worked.

But not tonight. Not even close.

Here he was, doing the right thing by JJ and her brother, making sure they had everything they needed to face the challenge ahead, and he felt worse than ever. In fact, based on the prickly knot in his stomach and the fact that he'd been awake for nearly 30 hours now, Alex felt he'd gone horribly wrong. *I don't know what it is I'm supposed to be doing here, Lord.* Every time he prayed for guidance, begged God for some kind of direction, all he got was a strong intuition telling him to "stay close." *I came back. I brought her home tonight. I should feel some kind of peace about that, shouldn't I? I should be fast asleep instead of sitting out here on this dock again.*

The light went on in JJ's kitchen, and Alex checked his watch. 2:40 a.m. The universal surrender symbol of insomniacs everywhere… turning on the kitchen light at some insane hour. The good sleepers? The ones who just wake up for a glass of milk or to get a Tylenol? They just work by the light of the open fridge. Only the truly hopeless go ahead and turn on the lights.

The hopeless. With something between a grimace and a smirk, Alex snapped on the boathouse light that cast a pale yellow glow over the dock. If nothing else, JJ would know she wasn't alone. He leaned back against one of the dock pylons, pulled out his ukulele and began to play softly. As he strung together random chords, he found himself praying for JJ, asking God to either send her down to talk or send her to sleep.

Ten minutes later he saw her figure coming down the path to the dock. She looked pretty bad. The warrior strength he normally saw in her was clearly fraying around the edges. "Couldn't sleep, even in your own bed?"

"I think I nodded off for an hour or two." She rolled her shoulders as if they pinched. "Not enough." She eased herself onto the bench that sat on one side of the dock and looked down on him as he dangled one foot in the river. "You play that thing a lot."

Alex tried to do a bit of a flourish at the end of a chord and messed up hopelessly.

She raised an eyebrow at the fumble. "You're not very good."

It was the closest thing to life he'd seen from her in days. "No, really, tell me how you feel." He modulated up two keys, trying to redeem his skills but tangling one finger so that a jarring dissonance floated out across the river. "Okay, I'm no virtuoso, but I have fun with it."

"Fun." She sighed the word, as if it were something forever out of reach now. He couldn't say he'd feel differently under the circumstances, and Alex was the kind of guy who knew how to have fun just about anywhere. "Think Max will have fun ever again?" she asked.

There was a hopeful, optimistic answer he should have given, but it felt like lying out here in the dark. "I want to think so," he offered. "No matter what they tell you, I don't think Max's life is over."

JJ slumped farther down on the bench. "Max is going to sue."

Alex didn't know what to say to that. He wasn't surprised. He waited for the defensive impulse to rush to the surface, the protective response to save Adventure Gear from what might be the most public and damaging lawsuit in the company's history.

"Aren't you supposed to try to stop me? Isn't that what your brother, Sam, wants?"

"Sam's a panicked idiot."

"It's your company, too. Aren't you panicked?"

Alex chose a new chord. "I hadn't realized it until just now, but yes. I am scared of what will happen to AG. Only scared isn't the same thing as panicked, don't you think?" Some dark and surprising place way down deep inside entertained the thought that maybe AG *ought* to fall. That shocked him. His entire life's work up in flames over something so regrettable as what happened to Max Jones? The thought turned his stomach to ice despite the summer night. Scared? Absolutely.

"Over there, they'd tell us fear was your friend. It did things to your body, to your senses that helped to keep you alive. They'd always tell us that when you stopped being afraid was when you got yourself killed."

Her words pricked him. He had stopped being afraid for himself, mostly because some part of him had stopped caring. Never getting in over his head had always meant not getting too emotionally invested, but when did that apathy take over and why hadn't he noticed before this? "Did you ever stop being afraid?" he asked. JJ had hinted at being in combat earlier, but this was the first she'd brought it up with any significance.

"Once. A local translator—a nice guy, friendly—went out of his way to help us. Gave us some useful information that could have gotten him in a lot of trouble with the local insurgents. It was the first time I didn't feel like

I had to check things out four times before I trusted the facts. I'd forgotten how freeing it feels to be able to take someone at their word."

In all his travels, he'd never been in a situation that called for that level of caution. "Wow."

"Yeah, I said something like that when the barracks went up in flames. He'd spent three weeks feeding us great intel just so we'd let him close enough to blow up our camp. So in answer to your question, no, I don't ever stop being afraid. Not anymore."

Alex began playing "Amazing Grace"—not in cheery chords but one lonesome note at a time. "I'm not here to blow up your family, JJ."

"You know, they all say that." Her hand went to her forehead. "Right before they light the fuse."

She thought of him as a spy? Plotting an ambush against her family? Ouch. "I want," he started slowly, not even sure where his own statement was heading, "to figure out what the best possible outcome of this whole mess is. Honestly, I don't know if that means your family sues our company into oblivion, or the studio pays, or what." Something about the tension in her hand, the way it clutched her forehead as if in pain, made him add, "I want you to come out of this okay. I don't want this to be another war."

JJ laughed—a dark, hopeless kind of laugh that echoed in the most awful way out across the water. "Too late. Max is back there fighting for his life and you want this not to be a war?" She angled herself up on one elbow. "You're the enemy. Well, you or the studio—probably both of you. You have to know that. This is the worst kind of war. Nobody wins this one, Alex, nobody."

Maybe it was the look in her eyes, maybe the lack of sleep, but her remark lit fire to something in Alex's gut. "So you've decided, have you? There's no way out of this horrid mess and nothing's left but pain and loss. That's how you're going to play this—like Max's life is over?"

JJ sat up. "You're going to sit there and tell me it'll all be fine?"

"No. It won't all be fine. But what's possibly served by you deciding it's all over but the penalty?" The ukulele hummed with the blow as Alex nearly slammed the instrument down on the dock. "I don't know what the lawyers are telling you, but every cent AG has—every cent the studio has—won't undo what has happened to Max's life right now. When I say I want to help, I mean something more than throwing money at the problem and pretending that that makes it go away. Can you stomach the fact that what I want might actually be whatever's best for Max? Can you give me enough credit to look beyond my company spreadsheet here?"

Her eyes narrowed. If she had a "war face," he guessed he was looking at it. "You really expect me to sit here and believe you have Max's best interest at heart?"

That was it exactly. No, JJ couldn't expect that of Sam—even Alex knew better than to expect that of Sam—but he'd always thought himself as Sam's opposite in things like this. As the guy who never made things about the money. He wanted to shout "Yes!" but even as he considered the answer he could see how impossible that must look to her. It was making him crazy that he had no idea what to do here.

"He said he wanted to die." The words were barely audible. Soft as they were, they hit him like cement.

"What?"

"This morning, when Mom was meeting with the rehab people, he looked right at me and said he wanted to die. And don't tell me he didn't know what he was saying because if you could have seen his eyes..." Her voice trailed off and he knew she was trying not to cry.

Even with all their problems, Alex thought about what kind of knife would go through his heart to hear words like that from Sam. He got up off the dock. "JJ."

"No." She put her hand out, tucking her chin down in determination. "Don't you dare."

"We're not going to let Max die. Nobody is." He ignored her stance, walking toward her even though she spread her fingers farther in defiance.

"Says who? What if that's what he wants? What if he can't stand the thought of living like some kind of vegetable? What then?"

"What if he recovers? What if he can make some kind of amazing life even if he doesn't walk again? We have no idea what's possible right now and..."

She raised the outstretched hand, and for a moment Alex thought she might slap him. "Don't! Don't you dare say *we*."

It wasn't something he thought about. It wasn't a tactic or a response or even a conscious choice. It was as if something pulled him beyond his own strength or wisdom, and he simply ducked around her arm and held her. She stiffened, but he would not let that stop him.

This wasn't a smart choice, but there wasn't any choice involved. She pounded his arm with her hand as her head dropped to his chest, her body still rigid and angry. Alex would have allowed her to hit him as many times as she needed to in order to let him close.

"Don't," JJ said, so much softer this time. "Don't." Her hand came down against his shoulder again, but this time it just lay there, lifeless. "Don't." He felt the heave of her words against his chest. There was a powerful anguish in how she halfheartedly pulled away, but he would not, could not relinquish his hold. He could feel how her jaw worked as she choked out a single, reluctant sob, and he tightened his grip around her, closing his own eyes to the swirl of pain that threatened to knock them both over. JJ pushed out the words, "He can't die," through what sounded like gritted teeth.

The pain she was in lit that old, familiar urge to run—to outpace the pain before it dragged him down. Instead, Alex tightened his grip. It didn't matter if JJ believed it yet, but he promised himself that running was no longer an option. Not from this. Not from her.

Chapter Eight

"He can't die." The words felt like they tore themselves right out of her beating heart, startling her. She hadn't even realized how much she feared losing Max. How much the threat of his loss tore open unhealed wounds.

"Hey, there," Alex said in this voice she almost didn't recognize for its closeness and tenderness. "No one thinks Max is going to die. I was with you when you first talked to Dr. Ryland, remember? I didn't hear anything like that from him or anyone else."

JJ wanted to pull away from Alex but couldn't. She'd been holding herself up for so long that it felt wonderful to be held up by someone else. Still, after a luxurious minute, she made herself duck out of his grasp and walk to the edge of the dock. "Yeah." She couldn't even pretend at enthusiasm. It was hard enough to get to a weak agreement.

"Yes, really." Alex turned her by one shoulder, staring hard. "What happened to you?"

She rolled her eyes. "My brother fell off a cliff, remember?"

"Not that," he scoffed gently, tilting his head to meet her eyes. "There's a wound a mile wide in there. Was it…back in wherever you were?"

JJ sat down on the edge of the dock, watching the reflection of the stars sparkle on the ripples of the current. It was easy to see why Max thought she'd find some peace out here—it couldn't be farther from what she'd known in Afghanistan. "I don't really want to get into it, okay?"

"Sure." Alex picked up the ukulele and sat down next to her. He began to play softly again, some silly tune she recognized but couldn't name. The rush of fear she'd just had tangled her thoughts. That, and her skin seemed to remember the sensation of his grip despite her every attempt to push it aside.

She tried not to talk, tried to let his music fill the darkness, but it was as if the story were clawing its way up, blocking her breath until she let it out. "Angie Carlisle."

She waited for Alex to say, "Who?" but he

simply paused the chords for a moment, looked up at her and nodded. Then he played again, letting her continue when she was ready. Her mom was always tugging stories out of her, digging for the cause of her moods until they hurt her, but Alex wasn't like that. Maybe, here in the vast empty night, she could let a bit of it unravel.

"Her name was Angie Carlisle. A bright, scrub-faced, too-young kid from Iowa. She died right in front of me, you know. I held her hand. I followed the medic's orders and told her lies that everything would be all right. We were in the truck, trying to drive for help, and nobody else would look at her. They stared everywhere else because we all knew Angie wouldn't make it. Only I couldn't *not* look at her. I had to look. Watching her was my punishment for the slip I'd made." Those last two sentences burned her mouth, burned everywhere as surely as the bomb that had charred Angie. Even though Dr. Ryland had proclaimed her the best person to deliver Max's diagnosis, JJ didn't think she could look Max in the eye and lie to him like she'd lied to Carlisle. In truth, that was as much the reason she was out here as the pretense of craving a night in her own bed.

"I'm sorry."

JJ almost laughed. How many times in the days she'd known Alex had she heard the words "I'm sorry" from him? They were all heartfelt, but each was mostly as useless as the last. "Sorry" just didn't fit for situations like this.

"That sounds really rough," Alex continued. "And then you come home, looking for a little peace and quiet to sort it all out, and get hit with more disaster. Hardly seems fair."

"Fair?" JJ spat the word out. "You still think life is supposed to be fair?"

"I think life is supposed to be an adventure. That God has peaks and valleys planned for each of us and we're supposed to learn from all of it." He stopped playing and shook his head. "That sounded so trite, I can't believe it just left my mouth." He turned to face her. "I really did believe that once. I think I still believe it, only I'm not sure how it fits with what's happening now. I can't work out how any of this would be okay with God. And if that's how I feel, I can't imagine how you feel." Alex set the instrument down again.

"That used to be my gift, you know—seeing how everything was connected. Finding the reason the problem was really an opportunity. I could find a way to turn anything around—anything." His eyes grew so intense JJ felt as if they looked into every last inch of her and saw all the dark thoughts, all the hopelessness she barely kept at bay. "But now I can't. I can't see the connection or the reason or the opportunity or any of it. And when I think about how it's ten times worse for you and a hundred times worse for Max..." He squeezed his eyes shut. "He's not going to die, JJ. He can't. He's got to live, to recover. He's got to."

JJ heard her own cries to God echo back from that dusty army truck. How she'd begged God to let Angie live, to spare her from the massive weight of guilt that had been pressing down on her since that day the insurgent charmed his way close enough to blow the barracks to bits. "It doesn't work that way, Alex. We don't always get what we want."

"We get what we need, right?"

"No, Alex. We get what we deserve."

JJ tried not to stare at the Gordon Falls fire chief. Her cousin Charlotte had told her the guy was new—and engaged to Charlotte's friend Melba, no less—but JJ couldn't help but be startled by the fact that Clark Bradens didn't look much older than she was.

He looked up from the pile of papers on his desk. "I think we can waive most of the training requirements given your experience." He looked up and offered a smile that explained why Charlotte had called him hunky. "I expect you've seen more action than a decade in Gordon Falls could dish up. If you're looking for a place where the only thing we blow up is balloons, you've found it."

"A little run-of-the-mill ordinary sounds nice," she offered.

"You didn't get it, though, did you?" Bradens set the papers down. "I'm sorry about Max. I'm the one who bought his boat, you know. He was a bit of a loose cannon, but a good guy."

"He still is," JJ shot back, feeling that gut punch she felt whenever anyone referred to Max in the past tense. "A loose cannon and a good guy, I mean." *Don't say his life is over,* she wanted to yell at people when they talked about him with *was* in their words.

"Of course he is—I didn't mean to imply anything." Bradens leaned in. "He's got a long haul ahead of him, which means you'll be here for a while. That's an ideal situation for me, so I'm glad to have you as a test case of sorts."

"Because you haven't had a female firefighter before. Charlotte told me."

"She also told me you're not one to shy away from a challenge." The chief stood up, motioning for them to head out to the apparatus floor, where the vehicles were kept. "And my guys will probably present a bit of a challenge."

JJ walked through the office door he held open. "If you're asking me if I'll pitch a fit when they cover my locker in pink ruffles, it's been done before."

He laughed. "Well, that's good, but I had another question in mind."

"What?"

The redheaded chief stopped and stared straight at her. "Are you running to or running from?"

"What is that supposed to mean?"

"It means that you've been through a lot. In my experience, if you know what you're running to—what it is you're after by coming to Gordon Falls—then you're a whole lot less likely to get hurt than if you're simply scrambling for any place that's not a battle zone or a hospital waiting room. I could really use you, and I think you'd bring a lot to the department, but not if you're using GFVFD like a giant emotional bandage." He paused for a moment before adding, "It doesn't work that way. I know."

"I'm not looking for a bandage," JJ declared, a bit more loudly than was necessary. "I gave you my paperwork even before Max…got hurt." She still hadn't found a suitable way to refer to the full-scale disaster that had befallen Max. "None of that's changed."

When Bradens arched an eyebrow—not quite in disbelief but more out of concern—she added, "Okay, I might need this a bit more at the moment than I did when I first applied. I think I need my life to be about more than just cheering Max through rehab, you know? I want Max to get his life back, but I need to get mine back, too."

"And that," Bradens said as he turned them toward the kitchen, "tells me you know what you're running to. You'll do fine. But I suggest you develop a taste for root beer. It's kind of the required beverage around here."

JJ smiled. "Love the stuff."

He pulled open a fridge that seemed stocked top to bottom with brown bottles of root beer. "You'll do just fine, Miss Jones."

Through the kitchen pass-through, a young guy in a sweaty T-shirt at one of the dining room tables held his fork like a microphone. Out of nowhere he began to croon the Motown hit "Me and Mrs. Jones" as he sprawled dramatically across the table.

"Sykes here is not known for his taste in

music or conversation. I apologize in advance for everything he's bound to do."

JJ was surprised to feel a smirk working its way across her face as she peered at the performance through the hole in the wall designed to disperse food, not entertainment. "Well, at least he can sing."

Bradens held up a finger. "Don't. Don't encourage him in the slightest." When Sykes continued his show, the chief slapped the light switch behind him and sent the guy into darkness. "Enough already. Save it for Christmas caroling." He pulled a chair out from the single small table in the kitchen and motioned for her to sit down. "So how are things at Max's boat rental and cabins? Are you going to be able to keep it up and running until he returns?"

JJ looked at him. "Thank you."

He blinked. "For...?"

"For saying *until* instead of *if*."

The chief quieted his voice. "Worried, huh? Well, I don't see how you couldn't be." His eyes took on a compassionate warmth. "It's a very serious injury. He's got a lot ahead of him. And so do you. Melba knows a thing or two about what that's like."

The chief's fiancée, Melba, was caring for her elderly father. Because Melba was a friend of Charlotte's, JJ had heard a bit about how advanced the old man's Alzheimer's had become. And how coping with it had asked a lot of Melba. Charlotte's grandfather also had had Alzheimer's disease, and it hadn't been a peaceful ending by any stretch of the imagination.

"You know, I was feeling sort of alone in this, but there are a whole bunch of people who've weathered crises like mine around here, aren't there?"

Bradens smirked. "There are a whole lot of just good, plain people who'd help out whether they've been through hard times or not." He held out the root beer bottle, and they toasted each other. "So yeah, you're not alone. By the way, the crew meeting is Wednesday night."

She thought of how good it had felt to let Alex hold her up for just that brief moment. Wasn't reconnection the whole point in being here? She wasn't alone—she was starting to believe that. "I'll be there."

Chapter Nine

Alex was so shocked to get JJ's call he nearly ran the entire way from the lawyer's office to the hospital. When he pushed through the door of the family lounge, he was glad he'd hurried. JJ looked terrible, crumpled with a box of tissues on the corner of the horrid blue couch he was coming to hate.

"What's wrong? What's happened?"

"I had to tell him again. I thought it'd be better, but it was so much worse."

"Max?"

She nodded. "He looked straight at me and asked me if he'd ever walk again." JJ pulled another tissue from the box even though she had a fistful already in hand. "So I told him. I know Dr. Ryland said we should feed the situation to him slowly, but I couldn't lie to him, Alex." Another tissue. "I couldn't. He'd see it in my eyes if I tried to lie anyway. So I took a deep breath, tried to find the right words and told him." She looked at him with red-rimmed eyes. "He was asking for the truth. How could I not tell him?"

Alex took her hand. What drove her to take so much of this on herself, to shoulder so much of Max's pain? "You couldn't not tell him. You did the right thing."

"You should have seen him. I thought he'd rant and rave, make a scene like Max is so good at doing. That boy has a mouth on him that could curl your hair. But no. He didn't say anything. Not a single word." She ran her free hand down her face as if to wipe away the image. "He just shut his eyes and gave up. You could see it in his face, Alex—he gave up. Like he didn't think living was going to be worth the effort anymore."

Alex caught her other hand and held them both now, giving them a reassuring squeeze. "He just got awful news. Really, I don't see how he could have reacted any other way."

"Max? Max is a master at reacting. At over-reacting. I was expecting Mount Max to erupt. Dr. Ryland told me they need to see fight left in him, and I told him that that wouldn't be a problem." JJ caught Alex's gaze. "There was no fight in there at all. It's like it wasn't even Max."

Alex searched for some way to reframe the experience for JJ. "His body's been though this incredible trauma. Maybe he can't have fight in him just yet. Maybe wanting to…to give up…is a perfectly natural reaction for him right now. Who wouldn't give in to despair, at least at first, if you'd just heard you're not likely to walk ever again? That doesn't mean he's never going to fight it."

That seemed to help her, even if just a bit. "I didn't cry in front of him," she declared, pulling in a bolstering breath. "That was the goal I set for myself—not to cry when I told him." She sniffled, then stared at the pile of tissues she'd dumped on the chipped coffee table. "Once I got out the door, well, that was another story."

Without thinking the better of it, Alex reached out and brushed a lock of hair out of her eyes. "It's done. It's better from here because now he knows. You've done what you needed to do, and I'd guess you did a pretty amazing job at a nearly impossible task."

"You think?" It was the first time she'd asked him for assurance. Mostly he'd just offered it, forced it even, but the fact that she'd sought it from him sent a small surge of emotion pulsing through his chest.

"Yeah," he said, smiling. "I do. Why don't you go tell your mom how it went and I'll see about how AG and the studio are doing with their side of things." His cell phone had registered three calls from Sam this morning already, but Sam hadn't bothered to leave messages so it couldn't have been anything more urgent than Sam's chronic impatience. "I'll say a prayer that the old Max will be back and roaring before you know it." As a diversion, he asked, "When do you start at the firehouse?"

"Wednesday."

Alex stared at JJ and tried to picture her under a barrage of fire gear, sweaty and sooty. His brain wouldn't create the image. No, his mind was too busy recalling the feel of her clinging to him on the dock the other night. "See?" he said. "New beginnings all around."

Alex felt settled, somehow, being here. The urge to run wasn't completely gone, but it wasn't yelling at him every second, either. It was a new beginning of sorts for him, as well.

"Why don't you ever call me back?" Sam's voice was filled with annoyance when Alex returned his call. So much for any settled feeling.

"Why don't you ever leave a message?"

"Maybe some info isn't the kind of thing that ought to go to voicemail. I need to be able to reach you, Alex."

"I was with the Jones family. I didn't think it was a good idea to cut out and take a call."

"How's Jones?" It annoyed Alex that it was caution—rather than compassion—that tinged his brother's voice.

"He just heard he won't be walking again. How do you think he is?"

"You saw him? He talked to you?"

"No, Sam. I'm not going into his hospital room. What kind of person would do that, even if they'd let me?"

"The mom and the lawyers are rattling sabers already, both here and at the studio. I thought maybe if you talked to him…"

Alex pushed out an annoyed breath. "Exactly when did you get so heartless?"

"About three minutes after Morgan sent his latest update. We might be solely responsible, Alex. There's a handy little clause in the studio vendor agreement that exonerates them from failures of promotionally provided equipment. We might not have solid enough legal grounds to go after *WWW* for damages, so if the Jones family sues us, we'll only have our own assets to call on."

"Surely a clause like that can't apply. They mishandled equipment they weren't even supposed to be using. We don't know yet if the guy on the belay line secured it right or used the hardware SpiderSilk needs, do we?"

"Morgan knows that. Only he says it's a lot harder to prove that than to substantiate failed equipment. Our stuff is physical evidence, whereas what the guy on the line did is only witness hearsay."

That wasn't good. "The cameras were rolling. They must have it on tape. Can't we use that to get to what really happened?"

"Of the three cameras running at the time, not one of them was pointed near that guy. They're smart like that. They cover their tracks. Which means we need to cover ours."

Alex didn't like the sound of that. "Meaning what?"

"Meaning you absolutely have to stay close to the Jones family and keep their anger aimed at the show rather than at us. The hit won't even ding them, but it could kill us. Even you have to have thought about that."

"Not all of us see the world through dollar-colored glasses, brother. I've pretty much only been thinking about what kind of struggles Max Jones is facing. And how to keep whatever happened from happening again. Ever."

"Yeah, well, if things keep getting worse, that may not be a problem. It'll be hard for AG products to fail if there's no AG anymore."

The thought had crossed his mind—mostly if the studio decided to do whatever it took—or cost—to deflect all blame to AG, not necessarily if the Jones family sued them out of existence. Honestly, Alex couldn't see why God would go to such great lengths to put him in close proximity to the family that would end his company. No, he still couldn't shake the unnerving notion that there was more to why JJ Jones had been thrust into his life. He just didn't know what it was. "Let's just all try to stay a bit calmer than that, okay? Watch what you say, Sam. I'm sure the corporate staff are nervous enough as it is. Has anything been on the news?"

"No, thankfully that's the one success we've had in all this. The studio has been able to keep things off the radar, and you know we'll do the same. It's Jones I'm worried about. If he or his family calls in the press, we're done for."

Based on JJ's account, it didn't sound like

Max would be waging that war anytime soon. "I think we're okay there for now."

"Well, make sure of it. It's a smart idea to stay close. But could you answer your phone a little more?"

Alex chose not to reply. He wasn't going to give any credence to Sam's idea that he had any intention of cozying up to the Jones family in order to save AG's bacon. "Tell Cynthia to call me. I want her to find me a few contacts for rehab experts in the area. Tell her to start sending my mail here."

"So you will be sticking around?"

Alex looked back behind him to the door, which had closed behind JJ. "Yes. I'm sticking around. But not for you."

He was sticking around. What a strange new concept for the old Alex. It made him feel a settled sort of nervous, closer to growing pains than feeling trapped. He just didn't know if he'd still stick around if things went from bad to worse—and they very well might.

"How are you settling in?" Melba Wingate offered a smile to JJ from across a box of soup cans. Everyone was working together on a firehouse food drive, and Chief Bradens had conveniently made sure that JJ and Melba wound up working the same collection table. On this beautiful Saturday morning, the crews were driving the engine around town collecting cans of food from the town residents while others packed up the supplies that the crews had dropped off or that locals had come in person to deliver. It felt every bit the small-town event, and JJ could feel tones of homegrown comfort and cheer soothing out her raw edges.

"I would have liked a smoother landing, that's for sure." JJ actually felt herself smile as a preschool-aged girl skipped up with a box of macaroni and cheese. The whole morning had felt spacious and lazy. "I feel like I've been running full-tilt since I got here."

"You have. I'm glad we finally had a chance to meet with all the running back and forth to Chicago you've had to do." Melba reached over the table to grab a paper bag from the chief, who'd just accepted it from an adorable family hauling a red wagon. The twinkle in the woman's eye as she touched her fiancé's hand was unmistakable. Those two were seriously hooked, as the captain used to say. JJ swallowed the memory that Angie Carlisle had been seriously hooked with another man from her unit despite clear regulations to the contrary. None of that truly mattered, as Angie had asked for the guy with her final breaths, and JJ hoped she'd never forget that lesson. "How is Max?"

JJ employed her now-standard answer: "It's hard to say. We can't really expect much of anything from him at this point, and it's too early to know how his injuries will play out, much less how he'll come to deal with it all. One minute he's calm and maybe even resigned, the next he's a ball of anger."

Melba lined up soup cans in the box on the floor between them. "Clark would say that sounds just like Max. They weren't really friends, but Clark bought Max's boat earlier this year, so they talked shop often enough." She lowered her voice. "I know he wasn't the most cautious guy in the world, but no one deserves to be hurt like that. I wish we knew how to help."

"I have dozens of people telling me how I'm supposed to be helping, but none of it seems to be of much use." JJ was startled at the sentiment; she hadn't realized how frustrated she felt. "It's making me crazy to just stand by and watch Max go through so much."

"It's always harder to watch, you know. No one really gets that until they have to watch someone they love suffer right next to them. Your cousin Charlotte's been a great friend to me with my family situation because she's been through it. She'll be a great friend to you, too."

Melba cocked her head and shrugged. "I'd like to be a friend to you, too. I'm in the thick of it myself, but maybe we can keep each other company in the trenches." She straightened up and winced, crinkling up her nose. "Is that a lousy metaphor to make to a military person?"

JJ actually felt a small laugh bubble up from some forgotten corner of her spirit. "It's fine. A bit overused, but in this case, it fits perfectly." She started another row of soup cans, genuinely pleased to return Melba's kind inquiry. "How's your dad? Did he hurt himself badly when he fell last week?"

"Oh." Melba's expression lost its sparkle. "You heard?"

"The chief took your call while I was in the office. I didn't mean to overhear, but it sounded like he took a serious tumble."

"He was so bloody. Honestly, it amazes me how one small cut on the forehead can make such a huge mess. There are days I'm glad I'm marrying a man who isn't fazed by that sort of thing."

JJ waited for Melba to make an additional battlefield comment, but she didn't. JJ was relieved, but she couldn't really say why. Maybe it was becoming okay for not every conversation to be about what happened over there or what happened to Max. Maybe that's how life outside of a uniform—at least an army uniform—grew into place.

Melba continued, "I suppose it's not too far from Max's case. Good days and bad days. And not much use trying to guess where it goes from here. Charlotte will tell you that kind of guessing will tangle your brain—and that's not a knitting metaphor." Melba raised a dark eyebrow. "Do you knit?"

It felt like an absurd question. A knitter was about the furthest thing from how JJ thought of herself. Still, she knew Melba was enthusiastic about the craft, and nearly every member of the Gordon Falls Volunteer Fire Department sported some cap or gloves or scarf that had come from the woman's handiwork. JJ offered a smile. "Not really my thing." After a second, she added, "I like to look at it, though, and all the guys love the stuff you made for them."

Melba laughed. "I think Clark orders them to love it. He denies it, but I have my suspicions." She closed up the now-full box of cans, writing "SOUP" in artistic letters across the lid. "I have no intention of making you learn. The guys make enough fun of me as it is and don't think I don't know how much of an uphill battle you've already got ahead of you with that macho bunch. Are they treating you right?"

"Actually, I don't think they know what to do with me. I know pranks and such are part of every firehouse, but no one's pulled anything on me yet. I think they can't figure out what to do."

Melba parked a hand on her hip. "Wait, you *want* them to prank you?"

"Not exactly. What I want is for them to see me as one of the shift." JJ reached for another empty box and started stacking cans from the truck that just unloaded its charitable haul. "If the chief can come up with another way to make that happen that doesn't involved stuffing my locker full of pink lace or ladyfingers, I'm all for it."

Melba's eyes went wide. "Ladyfingers? Really?"

"I've been trying to guess what the guys might do. Let's just say an internet search doesn't bring up comforting scenarios."

Leaning in, Melba whispered, "Do you want me to feed some suggestions to Clark? Maybe we can keep them down to a pile of pink ruffled fabric from Abby's shop."

"I think this is another good place for Charlotte's advice—trying to guess will just tangle your brain."

"You're a smart woman, JJ Jones. You'll go far in this tiny town—just you watch."

It was the closest thing to a welcome JJ had gotten yet, and she let herself enjoy the feeling.

At least until one of the firefighters plunked a box of Delicate Tea Biscuits down on the table in front of her. "Here, girls. We don't know what to do with these." He had a poorly concealed smirk on his face, as if he'd been working on the delivery of that line all the way over.

JJ stood up, delighted to see she came eye to eye with the older gentleman. "It's a food drive, Dave. They're cookies. You eat them, just like everything else."

Melba's smirk made JJ feel nothing short of victorious. "Uh-huh," the woman agreed as she accepted the box JJ handed her. "Very far indeed."

Chapter Ten

JJ was smiling when she walked into the firehouse two days later. Chief Bradens had called her to come in today to officially receive a locker and turnout gear. She was part of the Gordon Falls Volunteer Fire Department, and it felt so good to belong to something again. While she knew she needed it, JJ hadn't realized just how much until she got the call from Chief Bradens.

"JJ! Probie!" One of the younger firefighters looked up from a pile of valves and a stack of cleaning rags. "Heard you're in. The place'll never be the same."

His remark had a tiny edge of trash talk to it—the mother tongue of firefighters everywhere—but enough warmth to make JJ feel accepted. The catcall from the idiot in the kitchen, however, was met with her best "eye of doom" glare.

As she turned the corner to Bradens's office, JJ knew to be on alert. Firehouse "probie"—short for probationary—pranks were legendary. Hosings were almost par for the course, as were sand in boots, flour on cot pillows—she'd seen or heard most of the standard repertoire of stunts. Her vulnerability would be lessened by the fact that Bradens had been forced to do a creative bit of room shuffling in order to get gender-friendly shower and changing facilities. This meant the guys didn't have ready access to her quarters. At least that's what JJ hoped.

Although no one actually lived at the firehouse, there were a handful of cots, a bay of showers and individual lockers for everyone. The presentation of a locker key and a name plaque over a cubby for turnout gear was the GFVFD ceremonial induction. She'd already been given a stack of T-shirts—many of which were rather enormous on her—and JJ's uniform was on order from measurements she'd given earlier. Bradens had made it clear that the job was hers for the taking if she sailed through the training, and she had.

"Jones." The chief shook her hand with a wide smile. She liked that Bradens called her by her last name, just like he did with every other firefighter. "Got a few things for you."

JJ let herself grin. "So I hear."

Bradens nodded back toward the apparatus floor, where the turnout gear hung along a wall. She could already hear the chatter from the other guys, who were no doubt lined up. If tradition were any indication, she'd end up soaking wet at some point in the afternoon.

She noticed it somewhere just outside the door. A strong scent, as if someone had brought in flowers. Pushing open the metal door, it hit her like a dozen department store cosmetics counters. The scent of perfume—loads and loads of bad perfume—filled the place with a smell strong enough to make her eyes sting.

There were each of the guys, guffawing like six graders and sporting pink clothespins on their noses. Pink daisy stickers lined a little path directly to her equipment. Some idiot had covered her helmet in baby-pink ruffles with a giant plastic flower spouting from the top. Even her boots had been covered in rainbow and unicorn stickers worthy of a third-grade prima donna.

The chief actually choked. "For crying out loud, Davidson, I said you could have a little fun with this, not empty out a department store fragrance aisle."

Davidson responded with a snickering curtsy. "Your enthusiasm is…suffocating." He choked and wiped his eyes, which were watering as badly as JJ's were—and not from laughter. "Who's got the key?"

A miserable-looking Chad Owens reached into his shirt pocket. "And here I thought I'd gone too far." He produced a key that was so covered in pink glitter it blinded the eye, strung up on an enormous swath of yellow polka-dotted frilly mesh.

"That's my key?" JJ asked, not bothering to hide her distaste for the gaudy bauble. At least the hardware store could fix that quickly. She was currently calculating how many fires—or wash cycles—it would take to get the scent of bad perfume out of her gear.

"Looks more like a parade float to me. Again, which part of 'a *little* fun' did you guys not hear?"

"Sorry, Chief." Jesse Sykes held a hand to his ear. "I can't quite hear you on account of all the delightful *fragrance*."

Snickers and hideously imitated French accents filled the air.

"I expect even Jeannie can smell the gear

from here." Chad scowled at his wife's candy shop, which happened to be right across the street.

"I expect *Iowa* can smell it from here." The chief scowled even harder.

"I may actually look forward to a dousing." JJ muttered. The place—and more specifically all of her new gear—absolutely reeked. "I may hold the hose myself." She looked at Davidson. "You do know most perfumes are flammable, don't you?"

"It's okay, honey," said one of the older guys. "The fire'll smell you coming."

"What's a little perfume to a sweet thing like you?" teased another.

Honey? Sweet thing? Pink ruffles were one thing, names like that were another. Chief Bradens took a breath to set the guy straight, but JJ held up a finger. With all the command of a combat veteran, JJ slowly walked up to the first man, ignoring the "uh-ohs" coming from the men behind her.

JJ dropped her voice to a menacing tone. "You will never, *ever* address me by that word again." She glared at the other one. "No honey, no sweetie, no gal, no other such term, even if it's what you call your favorite granddaughter. Are we clear?"

"Sure." The first guy tried to laugh it off.

"I am absolutely, positively dead serious here. I mean somber, unequivocal, get-my-lawyer-on-speed-dial serious. Got it?"

"Yeah, I got it," said the second.

"I expected better of you lugs," Chief Bradens's growl came from behind her. "I can see we've got a lot of work to do."

JJ coughed and fanned the air in front of her—the stench from her gear was downright overpowering. She turned and accepted the ridiculous key from Chad. "Does it still work?"

He peered at it. "You know, I'm not actually sure." He rubbed his hands in annoyance. "The glitter gets everywhere."

"I hate glitter. Just for the record. I'm no fan of pink, either."

Chad frowned. "I had hoped for a better reception." He held out a hand. "Welcome to the department, Jones. You've got a long uphill climb ahead of you."

He found her out on their dock that evening, just sitting and staring into the water. He'd come to think of it as "their dock," which was startling in itself; Alex didn't attach himself to places like that.

He sat down next to her and offered her half

of the chocolate bar he'd just opened. "Mayan recipe chocolate. From the upcoming holiday catalog. You know how I feel about Christmas in July." He'd meant it to be funny, but it fell disastrously short of humor.

She broke off one of the squares—precisely along the scoring, while he'd just snapped off the first corner he could reach—and popped it into her mouth. "It's really good." He was almost going to reach out and hold her hand until she turned and assessed him with narrowed eyes. "Why are you giving me really good chocolate?"

It bothered him that she was so suspicious of his motives, even his good ones. "For one, I have yet to meet anyone worth knowing who doesn't appreciate really good chocolate. And second, let's just say I met Clark Bradens in the coffee shop this morning."

She didn't say anything. Just ate another square of chocolate.

"Don't cave now, JJ. It was just a dog pile of stupid pranks and old-school guys who don't know any better. Everyone's gotten them out of their systems now. You're not going to back down, are you?"

"Maybe I feel like another battle is the last thing I need. Maybe I need to drop this and focus on Max. It's been a tough couple of weeks, if you haven't noticed."

"Come on, that's not you. You're tougher than anything those guys can dish out. You know that."

"Oh, you know me so well?"

He did, actually, which was half of what was bothering him. He was brilliant in casting visions for people, in making them want things or come on board for a campaign. Suddenly he was close enough to JJ to see the emotions and motivations behind her actions—and that felt too close for comfort.

"I think even Clark sees that you shouldn't back down now. He said as much to me."

"Did he send you over here? Do I get a whole basket of chocolate bars if I go back?"

Alex rolled his eyes. "Why is it so hard for you to believe someone might just want to be nice to you?"

She tossed the rest of the bar, still in its wrapper, onto the bench. "Everyone has an agenda, Alex."

"It's a chocolate bar, JJ, not a lobbying campaign. Look, I came here to make sure you were okay and weren't thinking of quitting because I thought we were friends."

That made her turn to look at him. "Friends?

How do you think you and I can be friends in all this?"

"So everything that's happened between us just goes away because things are complicated? Look, JJ, I admit I'm stumped when it comes to what you're looking for from me. I don't know what is happening here, but I'm okay with that. I don't need a game plan and I don't have an agenda. What I have is someone in front of me who I care about. I think she could be making a mistake, so I'm trying to help."

"Help? Or just keep me distracted from Max?"

Alex wanted to grab her shoulders and shake her. "This isn't about what's happened to Max!"

JJ threw her arms wide. "How can it not be about what happened to Max? It's all about that. It can't ever be about anything but what happened to Max."

"It's about you, JJ. Wake up and realize that."

"You've got a lot of nerve saying that."

Fine. If she was going to be so blind to her own motives here, he'd lay it out for her. The least he could do was to say what her mother never would. "Nerve? You want to see nerve? I'll show you nerve. Look in the mirror, JJ. You act as though you fell off that cliff instead of Max. Your brother is a grown man. He's had a horrible blow, but he has to pick himself back up. Why do you think the rehab people told you to go home? Because this is Max's battle, and while you can fight with him, you can't fight *for* him."

"Did marketing come up with that line for you?"

She was so stubbornly infuriating. "Cut that out."

"How can you stand there and fault me for helping Max?"

"Because what you're doing right now is not helping him. Giving up your own goals to push Max in the direction you think he should go is not the answer. How is not getting on with your own life helping Max get on with his?"

She stalked over to him. "Max may not have a life anymore. Or are you too worried that it might be your fault to see that?"

It struck him with such clarity that his realization felt like a punch to his ribs. Alex grabbed JJ's wrist and shook it. "Max is alive. He still has a life. Dr. Ryland seems to think he has really good chances at keeping all of his upper-body function, right?"

"I'm sure that makes you feel better. A quadriplegic would be so bad for business, wouldn't it?"

This time he did grab her shoulder. "He's

not dead. He's not dying. His life is changed forever, but it's still his life. This isn't Angie Carlisle all over again, and you're hurting Max by making it about how you can't save him."

"That was low, even for you. You should just leave."

The tone in her voice dug under his skin, and his frustration boiled over. "I can't!"

"Of course you can. You're Alex Cushman—it's what you're all about, isn't it? Escape?"

He had thought about leaving. He'd already tried it, essentially, when he flew to Denver. The old Alex would have been long gone days ago, especially after those blowouts with Sam. Still, he couldn't. He didn't want to. He was tied to this somehow, in a way he couldn't name but couldn't ignore.

He saw it, then, in her eyes. So clearly that he wondered how he had missed it earlier: JJ was waiting for him to leave. Watching for him to betray her in the way she had been betrayed before.

It settled on him like an avalanche. This was no longer about injury or money or any of those things. This was about him and her, about whether he would stand by her or leave. About whether he was even capable of standing by her, of earning her trust, of walking this journey God had clearly placed before him.

"I can't leave." It wasn't even close to an explanation, but he didn't even know himself what was going on inside him. He only knew that JJ was daring him to be like everyone else in her life, to show his true colors and betray her trust.

"Why?"

"You really don't know the answer to that?" The part of him that still wanted to leave—the instinctive impulse of the old Alex—burned dark and shameful. It was overpowered, however, by the part of him that knew—deep down inexplicably knew—that he could go clear around the globe and not escape JJ Jones.

Her face flushed. She walked to the edge of the dock and turned from him, hiding. "Why would I ask a question I know the answer to?"

Adventure Gear's eloquent visionary should have had a clever answer to that. Something pithy and dashing. Instead, Alex only managed to stand there staring until she turned around. JJ tried hard not to look him in the eye, but the more she dodged him, the stronger his conviction became. "Because I'm supposed to stay." And then, even though it felt like jumping off a cliff to do so, Alex made himself add, "And because I want to stay."

Her eyes widened and she backed up against the lamppost. "Max doesn't need you."

The panic he'd felt a second ago evaporated, replaced by a resolve that was as strong as it was surprising. He took a step toward her. "I'm not staying for Max." He reached for her hand.

At first JJ edged out of his grasp, but when he took another step, she stilled her hand and let him grasp it. She was such a warrior to everyone else, yet he could see her wounds with such clarity. He waited until her hand softened, waited until her eyes stopped darting around the riverbank and settled into his gaze.

The world had taught her never to trust.

God had placed him here to undo that lesson, even in this tangled mess.

"I'm staying for you. Because I don't think we've lost the two people who talked all night on this dock. Not yet. I want that back, and I'm willing to fight for it to come back."

"They're gone." The loss in her voice let Alex know those nights had meant as much to her as they did to him. "Bing and Rosemary are gone."

Alex shook his head as he took her other hand and stepped closer. "No. I don't believe that. They're just Alex and JJ now, and we need to figure out how that works." He ran one finger down the curve of her cheek, his own heart slamming against his chest as he heard her breath catch. "I don't know how to do this, but I know I want to try. I know I have to try." He let his fingers slide to the softness of her neck, delighting in how her response to his touch played in her eyes. "The only thing I am sure of is that I could go anywhere in the world and still think of you. I'm supposed to be here, JJ. You're the one who's supposed to teach me how to stay."

"And what do you teach me?" Her voice was whisper soft, tentative, yet full of wonder.

The way she looked at him in that moment, Alex wanted to fly her around the globe and show her every beautiful thing the world had to offer. He leaned in and kissed her. A single small kiss that was more of a gentle promise than a display of the thunder in his heart. "I teach you that not everyone is out to hurt you."

He pulled her into his arms, delighted that she offered no resistance. "And maybe I can help you come up with a way to put the fire-house guys in their place. After all, I'm known for my creative ideas."

Chapter Eleven

The next day, JJ walked into the firehouse meeting with a huge jug of laundry soap and two bright yellow laundry baskets.

Wally Foreman, one of the station's lead pranksters, looked up from the engine fender he was cleaning. "Here to do the wash?"

She gave him a smirk. "Not exactly. Sit tight and I'll be back in a minute." Whistling, JJ parked the baskets against her hip and headed for the chief's office. She and Alex had indeed cooked up a retribution for the guy's fragrant fiasco the other day, and she was delighted that Bradens had endorsed it when she'd phoned him this morning.

The chief's conspiratorial grin when she knocked on his office door widened her own smile. "You ready to put those goons in their place?"

"Absolutely." She nodded at him. "And thanks. For having my back on this, I mean."

Bradens stood. "I'm all for fun, but they took it too far. I could lecture them on gender sensitivity, but I think this is more of a language they'll understand. Around here you need to give as good as you get, if you know what I mean."

She did. "Ten minutes? You've got the shirts?"

"Melba picked them up from the hospital foundation this morning." He reached under his desk to produce a brown paper bag and handed it to her. "You've gone up a notch in her view. She lost her mom to breast cancer, you know. She was going to try to get a walk team together on her own, but this is a much better solution."

JJ grinned. "Nothing is more satisfying than taking a nasty problem and turning it into a golden opportunity, don't you think?" She'd given Alex a little bit more than a kiss on the cheek when he'd come up with the idea. Creative solutions really were his gift.

Bradens checked his watch. "I'll let you know in ten minutes."

The company gave her no end of grief for the domestic props JJ placed on the table in front of her when they all met in the dining room a few minutes later. The wisecracks were predictable and rather lame, but they didn't really bother her. After all, she knew what was coming, and these poor lugs had no idea what was about to hit them.

The chief called the meeting to order and went through a brief agenda of standard business—shift schedules, new equipment on order, inspections Chad was doing that week, upcoming trainings. "Now," he said, turning to JJ, "our probie has a little task for all of you. One I trust you'll enjoy and embrace with all the…enthusiasm I know you possess. And by embrace, I mean this is now required. By me. Without exception."

That got the guys' attention. JJ stood and cleared her throat. "I can't say I fully appreciated the welcome you gave me earlier. Let's simply say it has lingered in my memory."

"And our noses!" Jesse snickered.

She continued, undaunted and even enjoying the anticipation. "Exactly. All my attempts to put that little stunt behind me haven't quite worked. I figure it will take eleven washings to get me smelling like a firefighter again instead of a perfume counter." She walked over and handed the basket to Jesse. It contained no less than a dozen T-shirts, two uniforms and all her turnout gear. "That's one load for each of you. Jesse, you get to start."

Jesse's eye popped. "I'm doing your wash?"

JJ handed him the jug. "And yours. I know I can't wait to smell like..." She made a show of peering at the bottle. She and Alex had combed the Halverson's grocery aisle until they'd found the most flowery laundry detergent. "...Lavender Sunshine, can you?"

Jesse looked at Chief Bradens. "You've gotta be kidding me."

The chief gave a smug nod. "Nope. The way I see it, we'll be the best-smelling department in the state."

A chorus of groans rose up, along with loud protests by several of the older firefighters.

"Oh, but gentlemen," Bradens continued, "that's not all."

"Isn't it enough that we're going to smell like Girl Scouts?"

JJ took that as her cue to pull out one of the T-shirts from her bag. She gleefully peered around the bright pink shirt as she watched the men take in the lettering on the front that read Real Men Wear Pink. The groans escalated so much she had to shout to be heard. "The chief and I signed all of you up to take part in the Breast Cancer Awareness walk the hospital is doing in August. I named our team The Fumigators. It'll be fun."

"That would be *mandatory* fun, just in case you were wondering," Bradens added, reaching into the bag and tossing a shirt to Jesse.

"We have to wear these? In public?" Wally looked mortified as Jesse held the shirt up to his chest to a flurry of whistles and catcalls.

"I think you're man enough to handle it," JJ added. "Think of it this way—do you know anyone who's had breast cancer? Anyone who's lost someone they love to the disease?"

"My wife's sister," Wally said quietly. The man's face changed completely, going from annoyed to serious so fast JJ nearly gulped. "So, yeah," Wally addressed the company, "what's a little pink for a good cause? I say we call sweetie pie's bluff here and walk in the dumb shirts."

It was the most backhanded show of support JJ had ever seen. When Wally cuffed her shoulder as though she were "one of the guys," JJ hid her annoyance and took it for the initiation it was. She'd done what she came to do: join GFVFD on her own terms as an equal… until the next prank came along.

At least she'd gotten a bit of her own back with this one. And she had Alex to thank for it.

* * *

Alex watched JJ leave the rehabilitation center from his table at the coffee shop where he'd been churning through emails. Actually, having an email argument with Sam was closer to the truth. He knew he ought to just bite the bullet and call his brother, but he couldn't bring himself to open up that floodgate of conflict today. Sam was being a first-class jerk, and he wondered what that was doing to the company atmosphere back in Denver.

As JJ crossed the street, it was clear her visit to Max hadn't gone well. By the time she slumped into the seat opposite him, he could tell she was fighting back tears.

"Not a good day?"

JJ pushed out a frustrated breath. "He's a mess, Alex. He's in a spot where every weakness he's got is his worst enemy."

I know the feeling, Alex thought. "Sorry to hear that."

"He's not the kind of guy who can handle this. He's got no patience, he's anything but focused, he's quick-tempered and pessimistic…" She ticked Max's faults off on her fingers until her hand balled up into a fist. "No wonder he's gone through three physical therapists since he got hurt. I love him and I wanted to sock him after half an hour!"

Alex grabbed the fist and uncurled her fingers. "Maybe it's a phase. I get the sense that all patients go through an angry stretch. I did some reading, and Max's reactions don't sound that unusual when you consider what he's facing. Anger is one of the stages of grief, and he's lost a lot of the life he used to know. Of course he's grieving."

JJ sighed, picked up Alex's coffee and peered inside the mug.

"I wouldn't..." Before he could get another word out, JJ promptly downed the brew. He knew that for the mistake it was and tried not to laugh when she scrunched up her face.

"That's awful!" she sputtered. "I drank army coffee and this is ten times worse. Is that even coffee?"

"It's a particularly bitter exotic blend I've grown to love since Africa. How about I order you one of your own? Something a bit more your style?"

"Absolutely." She stuck out her tongue. "I may need two cups of real coffee to get that taste out of my mouth."

"Sit tight, come down off the ledge Max pushed you out on and I'll be right back."

Alex stood in line, enjoying the idea of selecting the perfect cup of coffee for JJ. He knew a lot about coffee from his travels—too much, probably—but he didn't know enough about JJ to feel confident in his choice. He didn't like the way that felt. This tiny window into how little he and JJ actually knew about each other seemed to war with the instant deep familiarity that had stunned him on the dock. *It's just a detail,* he told himself as he ordered a caramel macchiato on gut instinct. *What we do know about each other is the real stuff, the stuff that matters.*

They hadn't had the luxury of learning one another's habits bit by bit. They'd been thrown into full-out crisis mode so quickly after they met that he hadn't even taken her on anything that would be considered a date.

Alex liked to date. He was very good at it. He could dream up marvelously inventive ways to spend time with women, but it was more about entertainment than involvement. He had fun, but he'd never really fallen for any of the woman he dated. Doc had given him no end of grief about his social life, but Alex had always made it a point to be forthright with women when things didn't click. And they never had. Now it was so far beyond "clicking" Alex had no idea how to handle it. For all his exploits, who would have thought that a simple night on a dock would be the thing to finally unlock his heart?

The thought stopped him even while he accepted the steaming drink from the barista. Had his heart unlocked? *Is that it, Lord?* he thought, a bit stunned. *Is JJ the one for me?* Their paths to each other seemed far too rocky for that to be true, but then again, maybe that's what made him treasure the relationship all the more.

Smiling, Alex turned the corner to the little window table, ready to present his gift of a cup of coffee to JJ. Only she was gone. There was no sign of her—no handbag, nothing. He looked around, stumped.

A spike-haired teen in a tattered leather jacket at the next table sat back in his chair. "Shouldn't ever let your girl read your emails, man. Even I know that."

Alex glared at the guy. "Huh?"

"Your laptop binged and she turned it to look at it. Whatever she read ticked her off big time, bro, and she was outta here. You two-timing her or something?"

Alex stomach turned more acidic than his coffee. He'd left his email up. *Sam.* Nearly slamming the coffee down on the table, Alex flipped open the laptop JJ had shut to see an open email with the subject heading "Max Jones."

Well, of course she would read that; he couldn't blame her. He scanned down the window to the text, afraid for what idiocy Sam had spouted now. It couldn't have been worse.

Things are out of control, and you need to do something. The one advantage we had was how close you were keeping to the Jones family, and now even that's failed. It's supposed to be your gift, charming people. I was tolerating your AWOL attitude because I knew we need that advantage.

We've lost it, no thanks to you. Read below for an announcement from Jones and see what I mean. How could you not know they were falling in with Tony Daxon? You told me they'd talked about their intent to file, but you never mentioned Daxon. He'll wipe the floor with us, Alex. The studio can take that kind of a hit, or throw enough legal at him to fend him off, but in case you haven't noticed, we don't have endless legal resources for that kind of thing. Morgan is pitching fits, and you're needed back here since it's obvious your sticking close to the Jones family hasn't done us much good.

Time to decide if AG still matters to you.

Alex wanted to throw his laptop across the room, but instead he scrolled down to the attached email from Max Jones. It was generated from Max's Personal Patient Page at the hospital, a web service designed to help patients keep their friends and family informed during treatment.

Alex sat down, trying to absorb the document as fast as possible. He knew from the cumbersome list of directions at his cabin that Max wasn't much of a writer. It didn't take a genius to see that a PR firm had crafted this update.

The cleverly worded "Note from Max" pitched a heartwarming human-interest story of two companies pooling resources to help an unfortunate athlete who'd met with a life-changing injury. The tone was cheerful, hopeful, cooperative—everything JJ had just told him Max wasn't. Alex wasn't surprised at all to see small print at the bottom that just happened to mention that copies of the announcement had gone to all three major city newspapers and four television stations in the Chicago area.

This was just the kind of ambush injury attorney Tony Daxon was known to be—creatively underhanded and full of media showmanship. Alex was sure it had been a true ambush, with no warning given prior to the announcement's arrival. If anyone had talked to AG, Sam would have been all over it and feeding all the details to Alex. It didn't take much imagination to see where this was heading, and in a disgusting, Daxon-esque way, it was rather brilliant. According to the note, Max was calling a press conference of sorts for tomorrow—just enough time to make it supremely difficult but not impossible for AG or the studio to show up at all, much less show up prepared.

If AG denied any of the support Max was gushing about now, the company would look terrible. If they didn't show up, AG would look uncaring. If they showed up and tried to set the record straight, Daxon could pick a fight and the press would have a field day.

It was a recipe for disaster—on every front—all on its own. But even worse than the press release was Sam's response to it. He'd all but accused Alex of betraying the company by not sweet-talking the Jones family out of this idea, as if avoiding negative consequences for AG was the only reason he was even in town.

And JJ had just read it.

Chapter Twelve

JJ pushed the money through the ticket window. *Get home. Just get home.* Bolting from the scene wasn't like her, but she'd been so wounded by the email she'd read on Alex's computer that thinking clearly wasn't possible. She clutched the train ticket in her hand and fumbled her way to the correct track. Gordon Falls was the end of the line—how fitting.

She hadn't stopped gulping down air the whole dash to the station—away from Max, away from Alex, just away—and once she'd slumped into her seat in the train car, JJ forced herself to slow down her breaths. She felt the same level of betrayal she'd known in Afghanistan. And why not? What was so different here? Someone she trusted had, in fact, been sent to lure down her guard. She'd been duped again. Weak. Stupid. Useless. She set her teeth in resolve not to cry, not to give into the tidal wave of pain lapping at her heels.

The guys in the fire company and their silly antics? That she could take. Obnoxious was better than malicious any day. But deceit? Well, she'd just proved how poorly she handled smooth-talking deception, hadn't she?

As the train pulled out of the station, JJ let her head fall against the window. *I'm so stupid. I believed him. I let him in. Why? Why did I let myself be hurt like that again? If I hadn't seen that email....*

Her cell phone went off, and she didn't need to look at the screen to know who it was. Of course he would call. Of course he'd have some compelling explanation, and he'd sell it like the consummate persuader he was. That's why she had no choice but to leave, to not give him the chance to wind his way back around her heart.

Turning the phone to silent, JJ buried it in the bottom of her handbag. *My heart. He broke my heart.* It was a paralysis as devastating as Max's, stunning her into thoughtlessness, unable to plan any response except buckling under the pain.

What have you got? Her commander's advice for action under fire came back to her. *What's available to you? Find your high ground and hold it.*

What high ground? She was back from war, poorly groping her way to a new life that wouldn't settle, coping with a brother who was harder to handle than ever. There was no high ground.

There's always high ground, she heard the commander say, his gruff voice filling the hollow panic in her head. *Even if it's an inch higher, take it.*

Max. *Max isn't dead. This isn't Angie. There's still hope for Max.* Sure, it felt like her heart had died, but that couldn't matter. Not anymore. Her high ground, this time, was that she'd discovered the deception before it was too late. Alex Cushman had been exposed for who he really was, which gave her the advantage. Smart soldiers took the offensive when they had the advantage. Max had a war ahead of him, and if there was one thing JJ Jones knew how to do, it was wage war. And now, if the reaction from Alex's brother was any indicator, they had a powerful advantage on their side.

Max had mentioned something about a new lawyer who had all kinds of ideas for how to get Max everything he needed to make the most of his new life. It had been the only time she'd seen anything close to optimism in his eyes. Revenge wasn't the noblest of motivators, but she sure understood the lure of it for Max right now. Max needed a fight, and she needed to be his defender. She needed to prove to the world—and herself—that she was capable of guarding something precious.

If she hadn't been able to guard her heart, then she'd make up for it by being able to guard her brother.

JJ fished the cell phone out of the bottom of her bag, noting with a sting that Alex had tried calling three more times. She deleted the two voicemails without listening to them and dialed Max's phone instead.

"Missing the crippled kid already?" He'd taken to using that ugly term, and she hated it.

Still, it was a tiny step toward Max's old off-color humor—the "don't drown" of the cabin rules list—so she let it slide. "Something like that. Hey, when do you see that new lawyer again?"

"You haven't gotten home to read my new post on the Personal Pages yet, have you? It went up just after you left, I think. Sorry, Tony asked me not to say anything to anyone until it went up on the site. We're blowing the roof off this thing tomorrow. It's gonna be awesome. Will you be there?"

"Absolutely."

"'Cuz when we're done, I'm going to be rolling in it. Ha! Literally. Look at me, I made a cripple joke."

JJ cringed. "Stop that, will you?"

"Nah," Max countered, "I'm just getting started."

Alex slammed the phone shut for the third time as he walked up to the reception desk at the rehab center. He tried to wipe the fury from his face, smiling instead at the woman at the desk as if he was merely catching up with some friends. "Did Miss Jones come back up here a minute ago?"

"Excuse me?" Her cautious tone made Alex wonder if she was allowed to give out such information. This was, after all, a medical facility.

"Josephine Jones. She was just here visiting her brother, Max. I'm her ride, and I think she must have forgotten something and went back upstairs."

The woman typed something into her keyboard and then peered at the screen. "Mr. Jones has had two visitors today, and yes, one of them was a J. Jones."

Alex was dying to ask if the other one was a T. Daxon but he knew better than to push things that far. "Yeah, JJ. Is she back up there?" This seemed the most likely place for JJ to come after what she'd seen. Without Alex, she had no way of getting home except the train.

"She's not come back. Maybe she's waiting for you in the parking garage?"

Alex was pretty sure that wasn't the case, but he smiled at the receptionist. "You're probably right. Hey, Max is using the auditorium for that thing tomorrow, isn't he? Is there a closer place to park than the garage? I've got some stuff for the press conference."

She peered into her computer screen again. "The one at 11:00 a.m.? No, this is the best entrance. Mr. Jones booked the room starting at ten o'clock so Mr. Daxon's office could bring things over, if you want to get here early." She offered an excited smile. "They said there will be television cameras. It should be exciting."

"A real media circus," Alex said, meaning it more than just a joke.

He went outside, found a reasonably quiet alcove on the sidewalk in the next block and braced himself to dial Sam.

Not even bothering with "hello," Sam let out a string of unpleasantries before barking, "And next time, answer your phone!"

"Congratulations, Sam. Every time I think I've realized what a heartless profit monger you are, you surprise me."

"Excuse me for trying to protect the company we've taken years to build."

Alex got right to the point. "I am not cozying up to the Jones family to protect AG interests. I can't believe you even think that's okay to imply. Especially in an email. An email JJ Jones just saw."

"What's Jones's sister doing reading your company email?"

Alex knew Sam would respond that way. "I had my laptop open when I went to get her some coffee and an email with Max Jones in the subject line evidently came up. It's not exactly squeaky clean for her to have read it, but honestly, given all that's happened, can you blame her?"

Sam huffed loudly on the other end of the phone. "If you bothered to even *read* that email, how can you take her side in this? They've brought Daxon on board. You know how that guy operates. There was nothing left of Vista

Bicycles when he got through with them. You want to be destroyed like Vista?"

Vista Bicycles had knowingly marketed a defective cycle that had left three members of a university cycling team with traumatic brain injuries. Some part of Alex had always thought Vista deserved to go down, although it had been an ugly scene for all involved.

Daxon, of course, had always touted the near-billion-dollar settlement as the crown jewel in his shady career. The case had sunk to ludicrously personal levels, exposing not only company faults but shredding the lives of the six men who ran Vista along with the two manufacturing engineers who had ignored the fault. If there ever was a battle with no winners, the Vista case was it. Daxon was surely anticipating topping his previous record with a company as large as AG and a studio pocket to empty to boot.

"No, I don't want us to go down like Vista. I don't want Daxon involved any more than you do. But come on, Sam, did you really think I was cozying up to the Joneses for some kind of strategic advantage? Is that the kind of person you take me for?"

"You were…"

Alex cut him off, the very image of JJ reading that directive from Sam fueling his anger. "Because that's exactly the kind of person JJ now thinks I am, thanks to your email. That's not me. It's not *anything close* to me and you of all people should know that." A passerby stared at Alex, and he realized he was yelling into his phone. He tried to calm his voice, but the anger and the strong coffee made him feel like he had a volcano inside. "It's beyond what I can take, Sam. You are so far from the partner I wanted to build AG with that I can't stand it anymore. This is why I took that leave. This is exactly why I felt like I had to get out of there."

"Yeah, the guy who's always on the run is exactly who you are. You romp around the world, playing adventurer. My brother the global do-gooder. Somebody had to stay behind and cut the deals that pay the bills, little brother, and it sure hasn't been you. Do you know what our second-quarter profits would have been without that deal from Wander Footwear? They wouldn't get you to New Jersey, much less to New Delhi. Thanks for rescheduling that without talking to me, by the way."

Alex squinted his eyes shut and held his forehead with one hand, leaning against the wall of the building. The conversation was bad enough without feeling like he was hemmed in by concrete walls on all sides. When had things deteriorated to this? "They were fine with meeting next month, Sam. And we wouldn't have those vendors at all if I hadn't spent a year courting them. Since when do you give a hoot about my travel schedule? I'd planned this as vacation time anyway. I'm not even supposed to be there."

Alex could hear Sam slam something on the desk. "You *are* supposed to be here. That's the whole argument, for crying out loud. Get back on board, Alex, or get out. I can't take this half-baked commitment anymore."

They'd argued about Alex's commitment to AG dozens of times over the past months, and Sam had said all kinds of things. This was the first time, however, Sam had told him to get out. The words hit him like the slab of concrete he was leaning against—cold and lifeless. Alex thought of half a dozen clever comebacks but ended up just hanging up the phone in disgust. "Getting out" had never looked so attractive. Trouble was, based on that last conversation, Alex now knew what he'd long suspected: if he left AG in Sam's control, everything he'd built in AG's name would soon be gone. The company's integrity would go down in flames in a matter of months.

Maybe AG didn't need Daxon to take them down—right now it felt like AG was headed down all on its own. Trouble was, no matter how he tried to dismiss it, Alex knew that if he let it happen, a huge chunk of himself would go down with it.

He stared at his reflection in the building's dark glass, waiting for it to hurt. Thinking he should grieve the death of AG because it was already starting to die. There was certainly pain in the reflection, but it wasn't what he expected. AG's demise stung, but JJ's scorn pierced him much harder. If he could only fix one thing right now, it had to be JJ, not AG.

Pulling up the train schedule on his smartphone, Alex saw that a train had left twenty minutes ago. That gave JJ more than enough time to dash out of the coffee shop and hop on it, which she must have done. Short of renting a car—or a helicopter—there wasn't another way back to Gordon Falls. If he floored it, he could still beat her back even with her head start. And he would. He'd be waiting on the platform when she got off and he'd make her see the truth. He wouldn't take no for an answer, wouldn't let her go on believing he was the kind of conniver his brother had become.

Sam was right about one thing. It was time

for Alex to make a commitment to what truly mattered to him. It just so happened that that wasn't AG.

JJ Jones was about to find out just how stubborn Alex Cushman could be.

JJ had hoped the long train ride would calm her down, but it only gave her time for the anger to boil up further. She was a walking storm of resentment by the time she stepped off the train in Gordon Falls. Scanning the streets, trying to remember which one led home, JJ felt as if she could run there at a full sprint and still not burn off all the betrayal steaming in her lungs. As she stepped off the platform, she spied the last thing she wanted to see: Alex Cushman's rental car. Growling, JJ started walking the other direction. She'd go a mile out of her way to stay out of that snake's reach.

"Hey!" Alex yelled from the open car window.

JJ kept walking, even when she heard his tires crunching the gravel on the train station parking lot behind her.

"Hey. Let me explain."

That was the last thing she needed. "Oh, I think your brother, Sam, has done all the explaining I'll ever need, thanks." She didn't allow herself to even look at him. "Leave me alone."

Alex gunned the engine to pull in front of her, heading her off. When she tried to walk around the car, he got out and reached for her arm. "What you read…"

"Is all I need to know. And trust me, it's more than enough."

Alex stood in front of her. "It's wrong. What you read is not the truth. Not about me." How did he make his voice sound so convincingly desperate? Did they teach that in business school?

"It sounded a lot like truth to me. And it explains so much. Wow, Cushman, you're a real asset to the company."

"Did you even bother to read further back? The email Sam's message was in reply to? Or are you simply going to judge me by the words my brother puts into my mouth?"

That stopped her. She'd been so blindsided by what she read in Sam's passage that she hadn't bothered to read any further. Although, really, what could he possibly say to undo what she'd seen? Hadn't he already proved his skill for pulling down her guard? JJ stopped walking but didn't offer a reply.

"And, please," he said, looking genuinely

pained, "don't call me Cushman. I'm Alex. I've always been Alex—I haven't changed."

Now there was more fuel for the fire. "Except when you were Bing. Who was it who suggested keeping names and backgrounds out of this?"

Alex put his hands to his forehead, squinting his eyes shut. JJ had to give him points for good acting; he looked genuinely distressed. "Okay, look, I admit things don't exactly add up in my favor here." He put his hands down and stared at her. JJ ignored what the look in his eyes did to her stomach. The man was a master salesman—she couldn't forget that.

"Yes," he admitted, "Sam had the stupid idea that I should stay close to you and Max to keep things from getting adversarial. But if you read through the rest of that email, if you'd have heard any of our phone conversations since Max fell, you'd know I thought the whole plan of his was vile and underhanded. I don't do business that way. My arguments with Sam—the whole reason I was taking time off from AG—were over the fact that I can no longer stand the way he does business. I did not, nor would I ever, offer my support to you purely in the name of company interest."

JJ crossed her arms over her chest. "But

should it happen to line up nicely with company interests…?"

"It didn't factor in!" Alex shouted. "I don't think that way. Come on, JJ, you know me."

"Do I?" She allowed the words to contain all the snarl boiling up inside her right now.

"Yes. You do. Don't let one stupid, misguided email undo all the time we've spent together." Alex grabbed her hand. "Look at me. I mean, *really look at me,* JJ. Was what went on between us manufactured? Do you really believe I could fake this? That I'd want to?"

He was already doing it. Alex was already pulling down her defenses even though she'd seen clear evidence of what had really transpired. JJ could no longer trust her emotions here—Alex had shown her that.

"I believe Alex Cushman could sell anything to anybody and make them believe they'd wanted it their whole lives."

Alex slammed his hand onto the roof of his SUV so hard JJ was surprised it didn't leave a dent. "You won't see! You're so sure someone else has duped you that you won't even open your eyes!" He glared at her, his eyes dark and cold. "Max is the one getting duped, JJ. I know this Daxon guy, JJ, I've watched him dismantle companies and lives. He's all about money.

He's not about justice, and trust me, he doesn't play fair."

"Nothing's fair about what happened to Max."

"I'm not opposed to your brother getting compensation for what's happened to him. I'm absolutely in favor of it. But this won't be a straightforward settlement—things just went to another level. Daxon is a predator. Give him a loose cannon like your brother and he'll do so much damage your jaw will drop. I don't want to see you and your family dragged over the coals, but that's exactly what Daxon will do."

"Your equipment was supposed to protect him and it didn't," JJ shot back. "AG is still partially responsible. This announcement says you're going to take care of him." She narrowed her eyes. "Are you?"

"No one even knows what that means yet. No one's even had that conversation. How can Max say he's making an announcement if there's nothing to announce? Can't you see what's happening?"

"I just asked you a very simple question with a very obvious answer. *Are you going to take care of Max?*"

"That's what I'm trying to tell you. Daxon isn't going to see that Max gets taken care of.

Just the opposite. No one's going to come out of this on top with Daxon at the helm." He wasn't getting through to her, and that was kindling a panic in his gut. "Max is in bad hands. Ones that are all about the highest possible settlement and nothing at all about what's best for Max. This wasn't 'us or them' before Daxon's announcement—just think about that for a moment. Whether or not you trust me, you can't trust Daxon. This character is taking advantage of Max when he's vulnerable. Because…"

"Because you stand to lose a lot of money if he wins?" It was a low blow, but he deserved one. "You know what I can't figure out? It's why you're even bothering. AG is huge—you said so yourself. What's one bad profit statement compared to the fact that Max's life is ruined and no amount of money will get him up and walking again?"

"This has nothing to do with profit statements," he tried to argue, but she cut him off.

"Of course it does. That's all it's ever been about to you."

Chapter Thirteen

Alex knew he was losing control of his emotions. Everything about this situation was wrong and regrettable. He looked up at JJ, stung by the contempt in her eyes. She believed Sam. She believed Sam's stupid email over all the conversations they'd had together. In what world was that fair? He tried—without much success—to speak calmly. "I need you to believe me—this is not about money. Not for me."

She took a breath to argue but he held up a silencing hand. "Granted, it may be for Sam. But not for me. I won't let him turn this into a war. Daxon, on the other hand, is the kind of guy who will make this a media circus—one that will eat Max alive. Daxon won't trash Max's character himself, but he'll leave your brother open to attack from everyone else. Think about the *WWW* producers. They'll do their research, and they'll know how Daxon operates. They'll pull out all the stops to try to squelch him, and if the best way to do that is by casting Max as some kind of irresponsible daredevil, they won't care. The paperwork he signed gives them all kinds of license to make Max look reckless. Don't you think your family has been through enough?"

For a moment he thought he was actually getting through to her. That maybe Sam's interfering hadn't ruined everything. It didn't last long. Something hard and invincible came over her face—the return of the combat warrior. "Do you think I can believe even one word you say anymore? I'm smart enough to learn from my mistakes, Cushman..."

"Alex!" It was making him crazy the way she said his last name with such contempt.

"Mr. Cushman," she shot back, her voice icy, "I won't make the mistake of believing your impressive sales act again. You can thank Sam for tipping me off. I'm only sorry I wasn't smart enough to recognize it in the first place. If Daxon can back you into a corner to give Max everything he deserves, I'm all for it. I'll see you at tomorrow's press conference."

With that, JJ turned and walked away. No, she marched away like the one-woman army she was. A betrayed woman with a ten-foot fortress of distrust built up in every direction. A wall Alex somehow knew would now stay up for the rest of her life.

He sat there for nearly an hour, leaning against the car in the train station's gravel parking lot, wrestling with the clash of ideas in his head. *You can't fix this. You're the only one who can fix this. You've been handed a reason to leave. If you leave now it's all gone, all of it. There's no solution. Finding solutions no one else can see is your gift.* He'd never been so hungry to escape his life and so utterly unable to do so at the same time.

He reached into the car and pulled out his laptop, flipping it open on the hood of the car. The only thing he could think of to do was to read through Sam's email again and go over the statement from Max one more time. Those two documents had started the war going on inside him—and the one inside JJ, too, for that matter. He had to start from there.

The black and white of it all, the faceless black words on a pale screen, lent him a bit of perspective. The email was classic Sam. Sam's response in panic was always defensive. Alex, however, always met pressure with an offensive measure. Sam was reactive; Alex was proactive. Sam had responded in exactly the way Alex knew he would, expecting Alex to use whatever means necessary to protect AG. Sam probably didn't even find the tactic of cozying up to the Joneses in any way reproachable; he'd see it as the best choice in a toolbox of potential company-saving tactics. Asked to name Sam's response, Alex might have even predicted a stunt like that. It was only the cruel development of JJ reading it that had taken Alex by surprise.

He read back through Max's announcement. Well, not so much of an announcement as Daxon's "shot across the bow" fed through Max's Personal Patient Page. The wording was a dastardly kind of admirable…phrases of grateful surprise at how AG was going to bend over backward to help Max Jones. Not a single detail, just loads of expectations—assumptions, actually, because no discussions had ever taken place—that AG was going to go above and beyond what anyone could expect in the name of getting Max's life back.

It hit him halfway through the final paragraph: a demand was only unreasonable if you had no intention of meeting it. What if the way to call Daxon's bluff was to do the last thing the smarmy lawyer expected: capitulate? The impossible solution here was to find a way to give Max more than he needed without taking AG under.

Alex would just have to make sure that was exactly what happened.

JJ had just enough time to drive down after her morning training at the firehouse to attend Max's press conference. Chief Bradens had given her the option of taking the morning off, but she'd decided she didn't want to be asking for a load of special considerations so soon after coming on board. As such, she hadn't gotten much sleep, but sleep had been a rarity for weeks now, even without all the tossing and turning she'd done after yesterday's revelations.

The one good note was how much her brother looked like the old Max today…the infuriating Max who could fixate on something to the point of obsession. No matter what Alex said about the vices of Tony Daxon, the lawyer had done the one thing she couldn't manage: he'd recharged Max. Her old commanding officer used to say that nothing motivated like hatred, and it was true. If hating *WWW* or AG gave Max a reason to fight, JJ didn't see how she could argue with that.

Until Alex walked into the room.

This was a different Alex, a corporate Alex. He didn't need a suit to look like the co-owner of a million-dollar retail establishment; the blue of his eyes was bright and riveting above the serious black button-down shirt and crisp khaki slacks he wore. He walked in without greeting anyone and took a seat in the first row off to one side. Barry Morgan sat beside him—the odd attorney she'd met the first day at the hospital. Another dark-haired man sat on the other side. None of them talked, none of them even looked up, yet they managed to hold the room's focus. Was their presence the elephant in the room? Or was it the odd counterpoint to the slickly suited Daxon and his thin-faced assistant who flanked Max?

Just as JJ and her mom took their place as instructed behind Max and his doctors, four men in expensive suits and briefcases entered and stood in the back of the room. JJ was pretty sure they weren't the secret service, so she guessed them to be from the *WWW* corporate production staff. Max didn't seem to know them, but if some of the staff he'd known from the show had been in contact, Max wasn't talking. Daxon had instructed JJ and her mother not to accept any calls from *WWW* or any of its staff, either. Cousin Charlotte was there, along with some of

Max's therapists, and three video cameras and a knot of bored-looking reporters hoisting digital audio recorders rounded out the "audience."

Everyone stared at Max, who fidgeted and chattered with Daxon. Alex was right about one thing: it did look like a circus. If she hadn't seen the energy in Max's eyes and heard it in his voice, she'd have agreed that such a spotlight might bring out the worst in Max's high-drama tendencies. Still, she couldn't deny that the attention had lit a fire under Max, and that was far better than the sour resignation he'd had earlier.

JJ hadn't realized she was staring at Alex until he looked up and caught her gaze. They were the only people not looking at Max, and it made everything boil down to just the two of them. Alex's eyes were a thunderstorm and a beacon all at once. The number of emotions she read there—each fiercely intense and all seemingly focused at her—stole her composure. Regret battled with determination across his hardened features. He'd somehow dug his heels in—she could see it clear as day—but she didn't know where or how. She only knew that it had everything to do with her rather than with Max; the realization made her chest cinch and her pulse pound.

JJ did her best to pay attention to the proceedings, to hear Max's carefully worded statement and nod as if they really were his words. Only his family would know this wasn't how Max spoke at all, but this whole show was for the media, and even she knew media required expertise. Max spoke of his future extensive treatments and accommodations as if everything had been settled for weeks. She knew none of that had been settled, and the fact that Alex and the AG team—not to mention the studio corps—were taking furious notes confirmed for her that they were hearing this all for the first time. One minute Max was telling heartfelt accounts of everything he had lost. The next minute Max sounded like he was going to get everything his heart desired for the rest of his life. Sure, it was a bit disjointed, but at least Max was talking as if he *had* a future.

Near the end of his announcement, Max looked over toward where Alex was sitting and said, "I owe a debt of gratitude to the people of Adventure Gear, whose very generous settlements currently in the works are going to make a lot of this possible."

JJ was surprised that Max commented directly to Alex's attendance because no one else had even bothered to acknowledge that the enemy was in the room. Alex, however, straightened up with so much calm she wondered if he'd planned the whole thing.

"That's only the beginning, Max."

Wait a minute, Max and Alex hadn't ever met, had they? Hadn't Max told her that Alex rented the cabin anonymously and through a broker? JJ didn't much care for Alex's congenial tone.

"I'm here to confirm that Adventure Gear indeed plans to take an active role in your rehabilitation. We pledge to cover all outstanding medical costs and fund accommodations to your home and hand controls to your vehicles. I promise you, Max, that we will do everything in our power to ensure that your adventures in life don't stop just because they now happen on wheels. We stand prepared to commit whatever resources are necessary to ensure your full recuperation. For life."

JJ found herself watching Daxon's reaction carefully, but the man was nearly impossible to read as he responded, "I'd expect no less from a company with Adventure Gear's reputation for integrity." His words were almost—but not quite—a challenge. "It was a failure of AG equipment, after all, that led to Mr. Jones's devastating injury."

Now JJ's eyes were glued to Alex. Would he admit that much publicly? He'd always been careful to qualify all his statements regarding the AG equipment failure. Did anyone else notice the slight pause before Alex's response? "So it would seem. All the analysis isn't complete, but I stand by my earlier statement. We're fully committed to funding Max's recovery." That last statement wasn't made to Daxon or the audience. Alex made that promise while looking directly at JJ.

JJ had trouble finding her breath. It was hard to believe the rest of the room didn't stop breathing, also, but there didn't seem to be much commotion at all until Daxon replied from beside Max.

"A very generous offer, Mr. Cushman." Daxon reached into his briefcase to produce a single sheet of paper, nodding as his assistant went to hand what looked like copies to the reporters. "Only I can't say I find it so virtuous in light of this morning's news."

"And what news is that?"

"Only that a second victim has fallen. I'm sorry to have to tell you that we've uncovered another case. A young woman fell nearly to her death a month ago while climbing with AG equipment. Charity is a fine thing, but one does wonder if what we're looking at here is more damage control than genuine philanthropy."

Alex had originally planned to make that promise to JJ on his feet, but now he was glad he was sitting down. One part of him could easily believe this latest stunt was just for shock value on Daxon's part, but something in Alex's gut told him it might very well be true. He had the chilling sensation he was watching the death of AG unfold right in front of his eyes. Right in front of everyone's eyes, actually.

The whole room turned to him, and he knew his future was hinging on his response to this moment. It struck him as the oddest thing to be grateful he was here because Sam's response to news like this would have been to mount an instant denial. Alex knew somewhere deep inside that denial was no longer an option. AG was going down, and he was going to have to stand watch on the bridge of this sinking ship as long as he could. "I was unaware of that terrible news," he said, meaning every word. "I do hope you'll share the particulars with our staff at AG so we can take whatever response is required."

Reporters scribbled furiously. Morgan had jumped up and literally snatched a copy of the paper out of Daxon's assistant's hand, hitting what Alex could only assume was the speed dial to the AG offices on his smartphone with his free hand as he ducked out into the hallway. Papers crinkled, people mumbled and it was as if a small avalanche had filled the room with cold, alarming facts. Still, Alex felt an eerie calm. A hollow resignation of sorts, as if he'd already known this moment was on its way.

They'd lost already. AG would fall because people had fallen. It no longer mattered if this woman's injuries had anything to do with AG equipment or human error. It no longer mattered if AG fended off eight more lawsuits, trumped up or genuine. Daxon had planted the idea that AG was negligent with safety. The media would take it from there and AG's reputation would never recover.

Daxon would encourage this new family to sue, to jump on the momentum of Max's situation whether or not they had an actual case. After that, others would follow. The legal and image costs of multiple catastrophic injury cases would sink them, no matter the truth of any of the injuries. Climbers weren't generous with trust in equipment—and for a very good reason.

Max was making some closing statements,

looking up at his mother as she stood next to him dabbing her eyes. Alex could only stare at JJ. All the hate of yesterday had evaporated from her eyes. Its replacement was equally hard to swallow: a distant sort of pity. She knew what he knew: AG had just been delivered a lethal blow.

Some part of him was illogically jealous of Specialist Angie Carlisle, the dying woman to whom JJ had told reassuring lies. He wanted to hear JJ tell him it would be all right, even though both of them knew it wouldn't be. It couldn't.

It seemed so natural to walk up and apologize to Max that Alex wondered why he hadn't done it earlier. As he walked up to the young man it was as if the whole room parted like the Red Sea—except for Tony Daxon, who straddled the space between Alex and Max as if he stood guard.

"Nah," Max said sourly, "let him."

"I am personally, genuinely sorry." Alex said, extending a hand.

"Yeah." Max did not accept it, even though Alex had seen him shake hands with his doctors. There was no physical impairment preventing him; he was clearly choosing to deny Alex that civility. Alex wasn't even sure "yeah" constituted an acceptance of his apology. Was he really expecting one? The man's eyes were cold and resentful.

"I meant what I said." Alex placed his private business card—the one with his personal cell and email info—on the table in front of Max. "Whatever you need."

"Mr. Jones will need a great deal. And none of it will restore his former life." Daxon's tone was so filled with drama that Alex felt as if he'd just taken a bite of tinfoil.

He kept his eyes on Max. "I'm deeply aware of that."

"Good," Max said, pushing himself brusquely away from the table in his wheelchair, leaving the card where it sat. "Good."

While he wasn't sure it was the smartest idea, Alex ventured a glance in JJ's direction. Her face registered a combination of sadness, anger and confusion, all hidden under a soldier's veneer of control. A dark corner of him wondered if this was the face he'd get from her from now on—the warrior defending her brother instead of the woman who'd tangled his heart. Was she sorry his future was about to fall? Or did she see that as justice?

"I am sorry," he said to JJ, even though she would not hold his gaze. "I hope you know that."

She looked everywhere but at him. "Yes," she said. It wasn't really an answer—more of a dismissal.

Chapter Fourteen

JJ looked at Alex's slumped figure out on the dock and told herself for the fifth time not to go out there. It was better for everyone if they never spoke again. Daxon had, in fact, given the whole family strict orders not to talk to anyone from the studio or AG without a member of his office present.

Still, she found herself hounded by the hollow look she'd seen in Alex's eyes at the press conference yesterday. He took the news of that second gear failure as if it were a physical blow, as if he'd personally been injured. That kind of response couldn't be hidden or faked—that was true pain. JJ knew because she'd felt a blow like that herself. She could easily remember how it had shot a hole through her insides to know her mistake had killed Angie Carlisle.

It went so much deeper than military advantage or corporate profitability—it was human pain. Like hers, JJ knew Alex's wound would heal but never disappear. Daxon and Max were all victorious after the conference, too full of "we're going to make sure they pay" language to think of who'd actually have to pay the cost. Over them she could hear Alex's warnings that there would be no winners when this battle was over. The shadow over Alex's eyes told her he was paying already.

Why did we have to meet now?

She couldn't remember finally giving in to the impulse to walk out to the dock; she just sort of looked up and found herself there. He didn't turn around at first. The set of his shoulders changed—she knew he recognized her presence—but he continued staring out over the water. It felt odd to be out here with him in bright sunshine. Better, though, for the dock in the moonlight belonged to Bing and Rosemary, not to Alex and JJ.

"I'm going back to Denver this afternoon," he said, still not facing her.

JJ didn't reply. Really, what was there to say?

"Things are a mess. Employees are rattled, accounts are dropping like… Well, accounts are disappearing by the minute."

She had to ask, even though it bothered her

that she trusted Alex's answer more than the details Daxon had given her. "She really fell off of Adventure Gear equipment?"

Alex's shoulders sank farther. "Not the same set of gear. Certainly not SpiderSilk. We're not even sure the gear was a factor at all yet. Still, we have no choice but to pull everything. All the climbing gear. From every store. Even before the news services picked it up, it was the only thing to do. I should have gone back there earlier, shouldn't have come here, but..."

It was then that he turned to look at her, finishing the sentence with his eyes rather than words. His obvious pain made her consider saying "I'm sorry" for all he was losing, but that didn't feel right. Part of her wasn't sorry—no one else would be hurt now, hopefully. Besides, Daxon and the rehabilitation doctors had laid out all of Max's long-term care costs, and the figure was staggering. Without a sizable settlement from AG and the studio, Max had no hope of ever getting back on his financial footing. *Ugh.* She hated how so many figures of speech involved walking, steps, feet or any of the other things Max could no longer use.

Her face must have shown her worry because Alex said, "You'll be okay. All of you. Max will have the best of care and every resource. And you, well, I don't think the fire department realizes how good you'll be for them." He tried to laugh, but the sound bounced thin and lifeless across the water.

"And you?" It would have been better not to ask, but she couldn't help herself. Daxon had advised her to think of Alex and AG in terms of a casualty, a necessary element of battle, but she couldn't. Dismissing Sam or the nebulous office building she imagined somewhere in Denver was possible, but she could not simply dismiss Alex.

For some reason, Alex pulled a battered compass from his pocket and ran his ringer around the edge. "Oh, I figure we'll last through Christmas, closing down the smaller stores as we go. If we're careful, most of the layoffs won't need to happen until after the holidays. Media is instant, but legalities move a lot slower." He looked up at her, an odd determination in his eyes. "If it were just Max, we might have stood a chance. But with Melinda Taylor's case, too, well, I think the most I can do is try for a smooth ending."

"That's her name? Melinda Taylor?"

"Nineteen years old. Sophomore year in college. Geology major. She'll walk again, but not well. I don't think we had anything to do with it, but I can't really say. In this business, a little doubt is all you need to go under." He shook his head. "How did we get here?"

Hadn't she asked herself the same question? "I don't know."

"This isn't me, JJ." Alex sucked in a breath. "I don't let people fall. I don't cut corners or cozy up to families in pain for corporate gain. I don't lay off people I hire, and I don't hate my brother." He let his hands drop. "How did I get here?"

JJ backed up against the lamppost. The same one Alex had pressed her against when his tender kiss had poured life back into her arid heart.

"I never, ever stayed close to you for the reasons Sam said," he went on. "I can't stand Sam right now for even suggesting it, for letting you think it. I know you can't believe I'm not that kind of guy, but if everything else has to go south I can swallow it if I know you'll believe that...someday."

She no longer trusted her judgment about any man—Alex, Max, Tony Daxon, anyone. How ironic that the men she put her faith in at the moment were the guys from the fire department? "I'm sorry." What else was there to say? She couldn't give him the answer he wanted.

And she was sorry…sorry about everything, including how hollow and tired she felt.

Alex dragged himself upright, looking as weary as she felt. "I'm all paid up for the cabin through the end of the month—you can check with Max. I'll have to come back in about a week or so once the lawyers do their thing, but I'll stay in Chicago." He looked out over the river. "I loved our times out here. Funny, huh? I've been all around the world and this was the best vacation I ever had."

JJ felt compelled to add, "Until it blew up in our faces. That's the thing about bubbles, Cushman, they pop." She saw him visibly flinch when she called him Cushman, but she could never call him Alex again. Not now.

Her tone turned him to face her. "Don't let this win, JJ. Keep me at a distance if you have to, but don't throw that wall back up just because all this happened. Life isn't war. It's hard, but it's a good kind of hard when you let people in to make it all worthwhile. At least, I used to be sure of that." He shook his head. "I'd better find a way to fake that 'sure' before I get off that plane in Denver, hadn't I?"

Again, she didn't have a response. Life *was* war, every soldier knew that. It was just easier to see out on the battlefield, that's all. Alex was waiting for her to say something, waiting for some glimmer of hope that she'd find a way to believe what he was saying, but all she had now were doubts.

"Yeah," he sighed, looking down. "Well…" He was fishing for some way to couch this moment in optimism, to pull one of his rhetorical tricks. It made it worse that she could read him so easily now, made her ashamed of her earlier foolish belief in him. "I won't say goodbye." The defiance in his voice was forlorn. "I don't believe in goodbyes."

JJ looked him square in the eye. "Goodbye."

She stood on the dock, watching the muddy water swirl around the dock pilings, until she heard his car start and rumble off down the drive.

"Think of how much prettier we'll be this year." York—JJ was sure the man had a first name but she'd never heard it—gave a pathetic imitation of Marilyn Monroe.

Jesse cuffed the back of York's head from his vantage point directly behind the big lug of a guy. "Not likely, Yorky. You're still in it."

At which point the brigade started yapping—a high-pitched sound evidently honoring the fluffy pet Yorkshire terrier York's wife had insisted on buying once they married. JJ was surprised to find herself joining in, if only for a second before Chief Bradens, with a long-suffering scowl, held up a hand.

"Is it okay with you clowns if we get this done before sundown?"

She knew company photos were a staple of firehouse culture, although she was more used to them around the holidays. The connection made her think of Alex's lilting rendition of "White Christmas" as it floated out over the river that first night. Try as she might, images of those days "in the bubble," as she'd come to think of them, would invade her thoughts at the slightest provocation. Even when he'd said he was leaving, Alex hadn't really left. Every night as she sat on the dock, JJ felt the heavy certainty that her heart was broken. She'd known Alex had broken her trust, but she hadn't counted on how much more it hurt to know he had crushed her heart.

"One, two..." JJ pasted a photogenic smile on her face...only to shriek when a wall of cold water crashed over her from every direction.

"Wha?" She howled, instantly soaked to the skin.

Shouts of "Probie!" and guffaws surrounded her from the guys who'd clearly known to step back. As she wiped her eyes, JJ's glare shifted from Chief Bradens to his father, the retired chief George Bradens. George and Chad Owens waved from their perch atop the ladder truck, the "smoking gun" of a dripping fire hose in their hands.

She should have seen that coming. Dousing the probie at a company photo was the oldest prank in the book. She fumed at the reminder that Alex really had messed with her head for her to have missed that she was being set up.

Until she saw Bradens's expression. Hosing down the probie was a rite of passage. A normal, non*girl* rite of firefighter passage. The chief's amused grin told her why he'd allowed the stunt and even drafted his father and friend's participation: it meant she'd been accepted. JJ had become a member of this team. She belonged.

Finally, she thought as she squeezed the water out of her ponytail and accepted a towel York held out to her. *Right now when I needed it most.*

"I figured you'd be a good sport about this," the chief said as he handed a mop to Jesse and picked his foot up out of a puddle. "Because I expect you see it for what it really is." He lowered his voice. "You do, don't you?"

JJ couldn't keep the smile from face, soaked as she was. "Yes, I do."

Chief Bradens nodded. "It's a fine thing. A big step for the guys. Even if you did get soaked in the process."

JJ thought about the long, hot days in Afghanistan when a soaking like this would have been pure bliss. It was a soggy sort of happiness now, and she'd take it gratefully.

She let herself "soak in" the moment…until she watched a strange expression come over the chief's face. "Didn't you tell me Alex went back to Denver?"

"He went back yesterday. Why?"

Bradens pointed. "Then why is he standing in our driveway?"

She was sopping wet, laughing and beautiful. The knot that had planted itself in his stomach as he'd walked off that dock the other day, the one that had kept tightening the whole drive to the airport, the one that had twisted itself unbearably as he pulled into the rental car parking lot, was gone. He knew upon seeing her that the crazy idea God had given him was exactly what he needed to do. A crazy idea that right now seemed much simpler to accept than to try to explain it to her because her face darkened the minute she saw him.

JJ walked toward him, toweling off her face and hair but not the scowl that greeted his. "Hi, there."

"I'd ask 'Why don't you leave?' but we've been through this a few times before."

Alex stuffed his hands into his pockets. "I don't have the best track record of leaving Gordon Falls, do I?"

She didn't find that amusing. "Why are you here?" She nodded toward the firehouse behind her. "I'm sort of in the middle of something, if you hadn't noticed."

"They got you good. That means you're 'in,' right? Gender-neutral pranks are a good thing, aren't they?"

"I'm soaking wet, Cushman, and I'd like to go dry off. Is there something you need?" Her voice was all business, sharp with annoyance.

"I am going back to Denver this afternoon, but there's something I need to tell you first. Something I need you to know before I go."

Her eyes darted back and forth, suspicious. "I don't think there's anything I need to know. Not from you."

"You're wrong." The urge to take JJ and grab her by the shoulders, to make her hear him, burned so hard he had to fight to keep his hands in his pockets. "You're so wrong, JJ. Give me five minutes to prove it to you."

She narrowed her eyes, considering. He hated how she obviously considered him dangerous. Right now, he felt powerful, purposeful even—anything but dangerous. "Five minutes. You can choose to never talk to me again after that, but you've got to hear what I have to say. For Max. For you."

"Or for *you.* I don't have any interest in easing your conscience or hearing new rounds of how sorry you are."

Sure, he was still filled with sorrow over what happened. Only now he knew exactly how to make reparation. The solution was like adrenaline pumping through his system. He had to make her listen. "Please." *Come on, Lord, You know how much I need her to say yes. You know how much she needs to hear this.*

JJ twisted the towel between her hands. "I need time to get dried off. I'll meet you in Karl's in fifteen minutes."

That was all Alex needed. And while the crowded local coffee shop didn't exactly provide much privacy, he was sure he could make it work. "Great."

"No guarantees, Cushman."

"I'll take it. You won't regret it, JJ, I promise."

Her sigh deflated her right in front of his eyes. "I already do."

Chapter Fifteen

Alex stood in Karl's Koffee and waited. It felt like the first time he and Sam had opened the doors of Adventure Gear. As if they were standing on the brink of an enormous cliff, seconds before hurtling themselves down the side with only ropes to depend on for their survival. This thing, this feeling of risking everything, of being so certain yet so terrified—this is what he'd lost in life. It had struck him on the drive away from the airport that he'd kept disappearing to new vistas in the past year to find this feeling, this sense of laser-sharp focus. That was a mistake. The focus wasn't to be found on a mountaintop or in a rainforest; it was inside God's purpose for him.

Hokey as it sounded, Alex hadn't had this strong a sense of God's purpose in years. He felt ridiculous and unstoppable at the same time, and he needed to share that energy with JJ—and eventually with Max. Trouble was, that first leap off the cliff involved a very, very steep drop—one that would change his life forever.

JJ pushed through the doors of Karl's Koffee and slid into the booth opposite Alex. There was something about the way she looked in a T-shirt…thrown together, unadorned yet perfect. Wet tendrils of her hair still clung to her neck in fascinating curves. Even guarded and annoyed, her presence had a capacity to ground him and launch him at the same time. The power of his need for her to understand what he was about to do—and why he was compelled to do it—doubled with one look of her suspicious eyes.

"I'm going to fire Sam."

He'd intended for that to get her attention, and it did. "How? Why?"

"We're equal partners, so I'm not quite sure how yet, but the why is easy. He's become something—maybe he has always been something—different from what Adventure Gear was supposed to be. He and I, we can't be partners anymore. I think I've known that for months, but I just couldn't see how Adventure Gear could go on without both of us. Now I see Adventure Gear *can't* go on with both of us."

"What if he fires you first?"

"I've thought of that. I think he's probably thought of it, too. But here's the thing—companies, if you build them right, have a soul of their own outside of their owners." He pulled out his father's compass, needing something to occupy his hands while he tried to explain this inexplicable thing he was going to do. "AG has to have a character, a culture, that's bigger than just me or just Sam. I may be wrong, but I think the way I see things is more closely aligned with Adventure Gear's culture than how Sam does. Sam is a cunning businessman, but he stopped being Adventure Gear a while ago. I just wasn't willing to see that—mostly because of how my father saw our partnership as our greatest achievement. I don't think Dad would be very proud of that partnership right now."

JJ's glance flicked around the room the way it did when she felt insecure. "Why do I need to know this?"

"Because I've come to realize that Max's accident, the settlement, you, me, all of that is tied up in the same gift. It's all part of some radical, drastic opportunity."

She sat back. "I hardly think Max would agree with you on that one."

He was messing this up, allowing his desperation to communicate to tangle his tongue. *I need better words, Lord. Help me help her understand.* Alex pushed out a breath. "I'm not saying Max's fall was a good thing. It's a horrible thing. But I see now how good can come out of it. The whole Romans 8 'all things work together for good' vibe—I believe it. I have always told Sam that the worst problems were just radical, drastic opportunities. That's always been my gift. I just couldn't see how it applied to all this until yesterday when I tried to leave."

She crossed her arms. It bugged him. It was such a posture of defense, of disbelief compared to his own openness and enthusiasm leaning over the table toward her. "And how does it apply?"

Alex forced himself to take a deep breath. "We have to take Adventure Gear apart. Dismantle it down to the bare bones of what it's always been. And it's always been about getting people out into the wonders of nature. To enable people to go where they didn't think they could go, push themselves into places they didn't think possible, expand their horizons. Only lately, we've become about upscaling that experience. Fancy gear, space-age technology, luxury where luxury never really belonged."

"Sounds like just a lot of pretty words to me. I still don't get why I need to hear your business revelations."

Alex pressed his hands to his temples, reaching for the right words. "When I think of Max, I'm filled with sadness over all he's lost. Over what our ferocious push for new technology has cost him. I kept looking for a way to fix his world, knowing that there wasn't any way I could. Then, as I was driving to the airport, I realized I could restore his access to the world he's always known. I could give him new ways to be the old Max. That's what Max really needs—not a pile of money."

"Max's treatment is expensive. He definitely needs money."

"Yes, but not *just* money. Money is just the tool, not the true solution."

JJ grimaced. "You know, it's always the people with the money who say stuff like that."

The waitress came and filled their coffee cups, and Alex used that time to gather his thoughts. The moment had become so important to him he was choking on his own words.

"I see this as so much bigger than Max. I mean, it's all about Max, but it's about how we *all* move forward. Max, me, AG, you, everyone. There's really only one way out. The only way

Adventure Gear—the only way *I*—can make amends for what's happened is to make a way for Max to do the things he loves with the body he has now. It's the same vision I've always had for Adventure Gear, just with a new audience."

JJ's face changed just the slightest bit. A shade of the edge came off, replaced with the smallest spark of curiosity. That tiny spark lit Alex up like a burst of dynamite. "And not just Max," he went on, feeling the energy kindle again. "Soldiers are coming home from war with new injuries, new disabilities that are stealing recreation from them in ways that *don't have to happen.* Instead of taking all our energy and using it to create comfort or luxury or extreme access, what if Adventure Gear used that same energy to create basic access for Max and people like him?"

JJ's arms uncrossed. "Access for Max?"

He was getting through to her. She'd heard him. She might not buy into the goal that now pulled him along like a tidal wave, but she'd at least hear him, and that's all he needed for now. "Yes!" he nearly shouted, making people in the coffeehouse look up with curious faces. "Adaptive recreation. It's the solution for all of this. No one could bring to it what AG could bring. And Max could be on the crest of that wave.

Not just benefitting from it, but being part of it. I don't just want to give Max a settlement. I want to *give Max a job.* A purpose. A place at a new AG working to build an adaptive technology division."

She blinked at him, disbelief warring with a cautious hope. "Why are you doing this?"

He knew that feeling, had felt that for hours after realizing what he had to do. It made no business sense, and then again, it made all the sense in the world. It meant risking everything, but compared to the dead feeling he'd been fighting for days—months, even—it wasn't a risk at all; it was survival. He gave her the only answer that he had. "I have to."

Closing her eyes, she shook her head. "No, you don't. You don't have to do anything. You can walk away from all of this and never look back."

"No. That's where you're wrong. I can't walk away from this. Believe me, I tried. I'm supposed to be here. Now. Taking AG apart to put it back together in a new way, a way that matters again." She shook her head again and he grabbed her hand. She recoiled a bit, but he couldn't make himself let go. "I need to do this for all us. I want to be the man who shows you that some people can be trusted. I cannot leave things the way they are. You shouldn't leave things the way they are, either. This is the path that gets everyone to healing. I know it. I promise you it is."

Alex saw a tiny crack in the warrior armor, the glistening in her eyes he'd seen when she was desperate enough to let him in close. "You can't ask me to bank on this."

"Then don't bank on it. It's crazy, I know that. I'm just asking you to give me a chance. Don't write it off. Let me prove it to you. Watch me, JJ. I'm really good at what I do, and I feel like my whole life is riding on this. Just watch—that's all I ask."

It took her forever to answer, but her quiet "Okay" launched him in a way that nothing had in years.

"Okay, then." Alex felt like his whole world had tilted, but not one detail of the artsy little coffee shop had changed. Life was exploding on the inside, and the only clue was the small spark in JJ Jones's eyes. He nodded at her. "I've got to catch a plane. There's a company in Denver I sort of need to dismantle. It's going to be a big mess for a while, but the finale is going to knock your socks off."

JJ rolled her eyes, a momentary glimpse of the old JJ. "You and your high-drama words."

"Yeah," he said, sliding out of the booth. "You just watch." With JJ still staring at him, Alex walked up to the bakery counter at Karl's and slapped a fifty-dollar bill down on the counter. His days of upscale living were likely behind him, but he still had a few grand gestures up his sleeve. "Send two dozen goodies over to the firehouse for me, will you? The works. Just let the lovely lady over there at the booth know when they're ready. She's on her way back. Me, I'm on my way to climb a mountain."

The low reluctant laugh he heard from JJ as he left the coffeehouse? Well, that was pretty much the best music he'd heard in ages.

Melba picked a hot-pink feather out of her hair as they stood at the footbridge that served as the race finish line. "That was the most fun I've had in ages."

JJ chuckled at the memory of the firehouse guys running in the Breast Cancer Awareness 5K in not only their Real Men Wear Pink shirts but also outrageous pink feather boas Abby Reed had secured in secret. "They were all good sports today, weren't they?"

Melba held open a plastic bag while JJ tried to wrangle the unwieldy feathered scarves inside. "Except for Chad. Jeannie says we shoved him way out of his comfort zone. And with the way his stepson Nick was taking pictures, I'd say it'll be all over town by lunch if it isn't already. And then there's Jesse. When he started doing twirls over the finish line, I nearly tripped I was laughing so hard. I hope Nick got that, too."

"Max would have done something ten times worse, I assure you." It was an old reaction, a comment that wouldn't have caused a bit of notice before Max's accident. Now, innocent as it was, it cast a pallor over the happy conversation, stinging like a cut that kept reopening when she got careless.

Melba's eyes filled with compassion. "Hey, he'll be in it next year. I always see wheelchair racers in the big city marathons, so why not Max?" She forced a smile. "His wheelchair would probably be so tricked out it would look like a parade float."

"Yeah." JJ couldn't manage much of an enthusiastic response.

Melba cinched the bag and set it aside. "How are you? Really?"

"I wish I knew how to answer that." JJ redid her ponytail elastic and slumped down on the curb where they had been cleaning up after the race. "I'm good and awful. Feeling better and feeling worse."

Sitting down beside her, Melba blew out a breath. "Been there, believe me. Actually, there are days where I'm still there. I love Clark to pieces, and I'm so excited to marry him, but none of that changes the continual drama that is Dad." She leaned in toward JJ. "But this is a good place to have all that drama. People will come around you and Max the same way they come around me and Dad. It's a good place to call home, JJ. Clark thinks you're a fine addition to the brigade and I know we'd all hate to lose Jones River Sports just because Max isn't up to speed quite yet."

"I do like it here."

"You know, what *you* like does matter. I know it has to be all about Max right now—believe me, I get that—but there's a life for you here, too. And boy, I sure am glad to have some friends my own age around. And to hear Violet Sharpton tell it, you've made a few friends yourself. Just so you know, no conversation had at Karl's is ever truly private."

JJ sighed. "Alex."

"Talk about relationships with serious complications. I can't believe the whole situation.

There's enough blame to go around and nobody really wins when it's all over."

It was odd that she'd chosen words so close to how Alex had described it. "Well, that's the thing. Alex thinks he has a way for this to come out good for everyone. But with so many lawyers involved and Max on the warpath the way he is, I don't see how it can all work out." She gave Melba a short explanation of Alex's plans and how she hadn't decided how she felt about any of them.

Melba pulled her knees up and perched her chin on top of them. "Whoever said Gordon Falls was the place to live the simple life lied through their teeth, huh? I have to say, Alex sounds like the kind of guy who could make an amazing vision like that happen. No one could blame Max for wanting him to stay out of his life, either." She turned her head to face JJ. "Sounds like a job for yarn."

JJ frowned. "Huh?"

"Not yarn, exactly—and hey, don't look at me like that. I mean prayer shawls. The ladies' Bible study—which you should join, by the way—knits them and we pray over them and give them out to people who need healing or comfort. I think you and Max and even your Mom need a whole lot of that."

JJ wasn't exactly sure how some old-fashioned prairie accessory could work such wonders, but then again, who was she to argue with anything that sounded soft and comforting right now? The firehouse had plush teddy bears to give kids in emergencies, so why shouldn't there be a grown-up version? "Okay."

Melba grinned. "Great. What's your favorite color?"

A warm glow crept up from under JJ's ribs as she remembered Alex asking her the same question. She knew his was green. "Um...red?"

"Wow, you really are a firefighter. Red it is. And your mom?"

JJ had no idea what her mother's favorite color was. Her favorite sweater was a pale blue, and most of her cars had been blue, so that seemed as good a guess as any. "Blue, I think."

"Okay, red for you and blue for your mom. I'm pretty sure we have both of those in our collection. What about Max?"

Now that was a question. "I don't know. He's chosen a black wheelchair, but I can't see how that tells you much of anything."

Melba pondered. "Well, just black wouldn't really work. I'll give that project to Violet.

She'll come up something spectacular, just you wait."

"Well." JJ sighed. "Max has always been a bit of a spectacle." She put a hand on Melba's arm. "Thanks. That's really nice of you to do."

"I believe in being nice to friends. Even if my fiancé is your boss, I hope you and I will be friends outside the firehouse. Gordon Falls is woefully scarce in the under-thirty age demographic, so us whippersnappers have to stick together."

It felt so very good to be an "us" outside of the army and the Army of Jones. With a quiet sparkle in her chest, JJ realized she truly was healing. Maybe everybody was. Maybe the thing about Gordon Falls wasn't that everything was simple or perfect, just that it was borne together by one big community. If she had come here to relearn how to be alone, how surprising that the best way to do that was surrounded by good people.

For the first time in what felt like forever, JJ reached out to hug someone who wasn't Max or her mom. "Thank you. Thank you for everything. I'd like to be there for you, too, if there's any way I can."

Melba blinked back tears. "I hope you mean

that, because my family has a gift for calling in favors."

JJ's own eyelashes felt wet. Outside of the bonds of combat, she hadn't felt like she could rely on anyone lately. "I've got your back."

Chapter Sixteen

"You cannot!" Sam stood up from his end of the conference table, slamming his folder down on the huge piece of cedar wood. The enormous table had been built by their father and had once served as the family's dining room table. Alex had insisted it remain in AG's head office as a reminder that this company was always supposed to be a family, be about family, not some slick enterprise. That had been a nearly impossible atmosphere to maintain over the past three weeks. "We're contractually equal partners. And I don't think you can even say that, since you were ready to walk away from all this a month ago."

"Equal partners of a dead enterprise, Sam. Either we overhaul this from the bottom up or everyone goes under."

"I refuse to accept your proposal. I will not

have this company become some kind of pity factory—we're a retail chain, not a charity."

"We'll be nothing in another month at this rate. I've got three of the four vice presidents agreeing with my plan." Alex had already eaten his words about life not being war. He was in a full-out battle for the future of Adventure Gear. Actually, he felt as if he were in mortal combat for his very soul—despite how melodramatic that sounded. He stood up slowly, eyes locked on his older brother. "I'm not blowing smoke here. I will buy you out or fire you."

"You wouldn't. You can't."

Alex had been dreading this meeting since that day back in the coffeehouse. He'd always known that Sam would fight him every inch of the way. But he'd also known—with an unshakable certainty he hadn't felt in years—that this was AG's only shot at survival. His only shot at living with himself and with what had happened. "I can, and I will. I'd much rather make these changes to AG with you, Sam, but make no mistake—I'm absolutely ready to do this without you."

Sam looked around the handcrafted table to the faces of the company upper management gathered there. "You can't seriously believe that adaptive equipment is the answer to keeping

Adventure Gear afloat. It's one-tenth the market we had. It's one-*twentieth.* And upscale? No, sir. It's retail suicide."

That was really all Sam cared about, wasn't it? Not the chance to make up for some of the damage they had caused; not the chance to create products that would make a difference in people's lives. No, all Sam cared about was the bottom line.

Alex didn't even bother to address his response to Sam. The brotherhood they once had was forever split in two, no more repairable than Max's severed spine. Sam would never change his outlook; it was time for him to stop hoping that he would. Alex's primary goal now was to convince these upper managers to share his vision and move fast enough to save jobs. "No, it's not our full former market. But you've seen the data—that's already gone. We have to start over, and I'm convinced this is the way to do it."

Alex motioned to the stack of papers in front of each vice president. "Look at the projections I've given you. If we can secure educational and recreational markets—ski resorts, universities, vacation properties—we could grow the market far beyond what it is now. All these places would gain new customers if they could provide ways to accommodate for adaptive sports. Kids with physical disabilities have families. They have moms and dads who want to vacation with them. Soldiers coming home from combat have spouses and siblings, classmates and colleagues. No one is working to give them this part of their life back. No one is serving this market with the kind of creativity we can bring. And let's face it—no one is more motivated to find good solutions."

Sam pushed his chair away so hard it almost fell over. "I will not let you take this company on some kind of corporate guilt trip just because you're scared for the first time in your life. Your style is to disappear when things get sticky, Alex, not to latch on to some ridiculous pipe dream."

Alex was losing the battle to keep his temper under control. "The pipe dream here is thinking we can survive keeping on the way we have." Every day since his return to Denver, Alex had carried a piece of SpiderSilk in his pocket. It reminded him of what was really at stake. He fished the piece of rope out of his pocket and tossed it into the center of the table. "We pushed the product too far too fast and now we are paying the price. Our high-end customers aren't going to forgive us and the settlements will wipe out our reserve. We can stand by and watch while we shutter the stores one by one, or we can rebuild and keep as many jobs as possible. We can do the right thing here, people. This can be our funeral or our fresh start. And I, for one, don't plan to start wearing black anytime soon."

Tony Daxon stared at JJ as if she'd grown a third arm. "You believe him." It was an accusation of treason, not a statement of fact.

JJ pulled the door shut of the rental cottage she'd just locked up. It was the first of the month, and a couple was coming in tomorrow to rent the cottage Alex had occupied. "I'm not sure yet."

Daxon angled in front of her. "Yes, you are. You're just afraid to tell Max you're selling him out."

JJ stared down at him, glad to have even an inch of height over the man. "Does Max know you're here?"

Daxon loosened his tie in the late summer heat. "I thought it would be better to ensure I had your support before I handed Max this unfortunate offer."

"Unfortunate?"

"This is a dodging tactic. This is what Alex

Cushman is known for—the diversionary solution. This scheme of his can't possibly work. His brother's already left the company. Come on, even you can see this is just a way to get out of a no-win court battle. Offering Max a job in six months is like promising a kid in a desert an ice cream cone if he can just hold it for an hour. When it comes time to pay up, nothing's there."

JJ put her box of cleaning supplies in a cart on the cabin's deck and began wheeling it toward Max's office. She mentally counted all the steps that would need to be ramped if Max came back. *When* Max came back. "So you haven't told Max about the offer from AG?"

"I'm his attorney. I'm supposed to protect him from stunts like this. Especially at a vulnerable time in his recovery. Your brother needs financial security, not flimsy promises."

She'd seen the offer. Alex had sent her a copy. Alex had emailed her nearly every day since returning to Denver, recounting the gains and losses of his battle to give AG new life in the face of disaster. Reading Alex's struggle alongside her daily phone conversations with Max, JJ couldn't help but see how alike they were. "Alex's offer to Max was very generous. He wouldn't lack for anything if he worked for AG. And he'd have a job. A reason to get up in the morning. I'm not sure you can put a price on that."

"Oh, now it's 'Alex's offer.' I see it's become personal."

"It's my brother's life. It's always been personal. I wonder just how much you have at stake here, Mr. Daxon. Does the right thing for Max spell out in more than just dollar signs for you?"

Daxon scowled. "You don't trust me, do you?"

JJ put down the handle of the cart. "I've learned the hard way never to trust anyone, Mr. Daxon. Especially someone who declares very loudly that they have my best interest at heart."

"This offer is a mistake. Let me do my job here, Ms. Jones. Don't let sentimentality cloud your thinking."

There was something about his eyes. They lacked the clarity she could always find in Alex's gaze. Still, what he said made sense. AG's offer did hinge on their ability to stay afloat. "Answer me this one question. If we go to trial and we win the full amount you're telling me you're going to request, can AG survive the hit?"

Daxon balked. "You have no reason to be worried about what AG can survive." His eyes narrowed. "Or do you? Maybe it's time for you to think about where your loyalties lie. If it came down to what's best for Max or what's best for your new friend Alex, could you make the right decision? Are you ready to stand by your brother when he needs you most?"

The knot in her stomach—the one she'd supposedly come to Gordon Falls to heal—seemed to double at the question. Daxon had a point: it might very likely come down to a choice like that…on paper, at least. Alex seemed pretty convinced that his solution was what was best for them all. Was he right? Could she trust him when her family's future was at stake?

A month ago, there wouldn't have been any question, but Alex had changed her. In ways that could never be undone and in ways she wasn't sure she ever wanted to undo. "Are you so sure this has to be war?" She kept thinking of Alex's words, about him striving for the solution where everybody won instead of nobody. She was deathly tired of war.

Daxon's laugh was ugly. "Your brother is in a battle for his life and you, a soldier, are asking me if this has to be war?" He shook his head. "I have to say, Cushman is even more clever than I thought. He's got you hooked, hasn't he?"

"No." JJ's answer was sharp and quick and

uncertain. It was nearly impossible not to be drawn in by the optimism Alex gushed in every email. It was as if Alex grew more energized as Max seemed to grow more bitter. More focused on vengeance. Could she really blame him? She hadn't lost her ability to walk; her life had been changed, but it hadn't been blown to pieces like Max's had. "I just think it's a mistake not to let Max decide for himself." And that really was it, wasn't it? When it came right down to it, even if this turned into a war, it wasn't *her* war. Max had to choose how and when he'd fight for what he wanted, not her.

Watching Alex respond to the threat of his own life coming undone, tackling the disaster head-on with determination the way he did, had woken JJ up to a deep truth. Max could not be coaxed back into a full life—it had to be a choice he made for himself. With all the facts and possibilities, not just Tony Daxon's heavy-handed management. She squared her shoulders at the attorney. "So tell me, Mr. Daxon, will you show him AG's offer or will I?"

"I don't think it's worth considering."

"Don't you think that should be Max's decision?"

Daxon buttoned his suit coat back up. "If you want to take the risk of confusing Max with an ill-advised scheme that might rob him of the financial security he could guarantee now, I can't stop you. But you'll be doing so against my counsel. And you should know I'll strongly advise Max not to take it." He pointed a finger at her. "This is about Max. About getting him all he needs. He's an innocent victim in this—never forget that."

"I have a friend back in the VA hospital. Have you ever been there?"

"Occasionally."

"It's filled with victims. Guys who gave their all for their country and came back with injuries no one should ever have to endure." JJ had gone back last week to find one soldier from her unit, who had lost the use of his legs, hoping to gain some advice. Instead, the experience had been a devastating lesson in how war destroys its wounded warriors. She'd broken down and called Alex that night, terrified Max would end up the civilian version of the hollow souls that occupied the corners of those rooms. Worst of all, JJ had felt like she'd seen her own soul in those veterans—empty, burned almost beyond restoration. She'd always thought war had stolen her faith, but that afternoon she realized she'd been the one to cast it off, a victim of her own despair.

She and Alex had talked for two hours, clinging to a tiny piece of the connection they'd had on the river dock, reminding her that a faith cast aside could be picked up again if she chose to turn back. God hadn't left her—it was she who'd left Him. She just had to make room for Him in her life again. And that meant letting go of the despair. For herself, and for Max.

JJ glared at Daxon. "There's one guy who lost his eyesight and half of one arm. Only he's lost so much more than that. His every physical need is taken care of, but he's dropped out of life. Just sits there, waiting for the rest of his body to fail. Nobody's given him a chance to take his place back in the world. I can't help thinking Alex might just be handing that place back to Max."

"Alex Cushman is soothing a guilty conscience and a terminal balance sheet. He's already lost. He's just trying not to lose everything, and that can't be your problem."

"If there's one thing war taught me, it was that there's a huge difference between losing and surrender."

Come to Chicago and talk to Max.

Alex stared at the seven words on his computer screen, stunned. In all his emails back and forth with JJ, he'd sensed her growing openness. The night she'd called after her visit to the VA hospital, he'd almost flown out there uninvited despite his promise to Doc that he'd stay put until the Joneses had made their decision.

It had been hard not to bolt. The battle over AG had been bitter. Sam had been awful, and a few of the upper management had taken his side to make for a nasty split. Every day handed Alex a reason to flee the painstaking process of retooling AG for its new focus. He'd thrown his Go-Bag in the Dumpster at the end of the first week because it kept calling to him from the closet behind Cynthia's desk.

Cynthia was gone, too, laid off like many of the administrative staff. He hated Cynthia's loss more than all the others. She was a fabulous employee and someone with a bright future, but her departure had practical casualties, too—Alex was terrible at administrative tasks; the plethora of mistakes in his letters and emails had become a company-wide joke. Still, Alex felt it was essential that he bear the hits as much as any other AG employee. Too many people had to be laid off—and Alex hadn't slept well in weeks as a result—but the leaner AG would hopefully be nimble enough to shift and survive.

He'd be sticking around this time to make sure.

He found himself fighting his old nature with every ounce of determination God could give him. Even the travel photos in his office had to go because he found himself staring at them with a craving to disappear that often drove him to blurt out desperate prayers for the strength to stay the course.

JJ's email could not have come soon enough. The only thing that kept him from jumping in his car this minute was the knowledge that even a flight five hours from now would get him to Gordon Falls faster than his beloved Land Rover. He'd booked his flight and shifted four meetings in a matter of minutes. They were important meetings, but everything else could wait if he got the chance to convince Max Jones his future lay with Adventure Gear.

Doing right by Max had become far more than a corporate goal for Alex. It was becoming dangerously close to obsession—and Doc did not hesitate to express his concern. Doc's worries quieted down, however, when Alex admitted to his affections for JJ.

"She is not who I would have expected to

steal your heart," Doc said, his dark eyes crinkling with amusement. "But then again, that is how it always goes, mmm? She is a fickle thing, love." Doc could get away with saying corny stuff like that in his thick Italian accent, but then again, Doc could always see into Alex in ways even Sam never could.

"Has she stolen your heart, Alexander?" Doc had asked as they'd packed up the AG offices to downsize to smaller, more frugal quarters. "Tell me, has it finally happened?" Doc was also the first to chide Alex for his endless string of shallow relationships, so the Italian was rooting for JJ, it was clear.

"I think so." It felt both alarming and easy to admit his feelings out loud. Alex had always been passionate about life, but he felt close to very few people and never got particularly invested in any women. They were an amusement, a diversion, but never an essential. He'd never experienced the consuming yearning he felt for JJ, a craving that had only doubled since the phone call and gone straight off the charts with her email. "Only I don't know if I'm alone in this, Doc. I think I've won her over, but I'm not at all sure."

"Then it is good you are going back to Chicago," Doc had said. "There is no other way to be sure. That kind of assurance can only be found in a woman's eyes—not in her emails."

Alex had only rolled his eyes. He himself would have never gotten away with that kind of talk—not even with Doc's accent.

Chapter Seventeen

As he pushed through the doors of Max's apartment building in Chicago—he'd been able to move out of the rehabilitation facility to a nearby residential unit operated by the hospital as a halfway house of sorts—Alex thought of the last time he'd seen the man. The scorn in Max Jones's eyes at the press conference had never left his memory. He pressed the button for the apartment marked Jones, praying that God would grant him favor. He needed this. In ways he still didn't entirely understand.

Alex knew JJ would be there, but that foreknowledge didn't dilute the rush of pleasure he felt at seeing her face. The breath fled his lungs as she pulled open the door and her smile set off sparks under his ribs. A completely inappropriate craving to kiss her right then and there blinded him for a moment or two, rendering him speechless.

"Hi." Her voice was soft and a bit unsteady. Did seeing him send the same rush through her?

"Cushman," Max's deep voice came from behind JJ as the young man wheeled into view. He was using a high-tech, lightweight wheelchair, not the clumsy, generic hospital one Alex had seen at the press conference.

"Nice touch." Alex laughed as he pointed to the flames Max had painted onto the wheel panels. The outrageous modification suited Max perfectly.

Max managed a hint of a crooked grin. "Birthday present from a friend who paints cars. He offered to put a dual chrome exhaust on the back, but I thought that was going a bit far."

JJ rolled her eyes. Alex had so missed how she did that.

"Yeah, well, it's not like I can peel out of the driveway or anything." It had taken only a split second for the darkness to return to Max's eyes.

Alex obviously had a lot of work to do. "I like it," he offered to Max. "It's exactly the kind of spirit I want Adventure Access to have."

"So you decided on a name?" JJ jumped on

the chance to move the conversation forward, motioning both men into the apartment.

Alex shrugged. “It seemed the best combination of old and new. We’re still about adventure—just different kinds of adventure. And I’d like to think that someday much of the old Adventure Gear will come back into being.”

“Yeah, well, we all know about how plans can change,” Max grunted, spinning competently around to face them as Alex and JJ took seats in the apartment’s living room.

“How do you feel your rehab is coming?”

Max rolled his eyes—the same gesture as JJ, only nowhere near as endearing. “Everything takes twelve times longer than I want. And I only get half as far as I planned.”

Alex knew that feeling. “Rehabilitating a broken company doesn’t feel much better right now, I assure you.”

It had been the wrong thing to say. “I doubt that,” Max growled. “Not even close.”

“We ordered Max’s adapted car yesterday.” JJ forced brightness into her voice.

“Cost a fortune,” her brother added. “I could have gotten a top-of-the-line Mustang for what we’ll be dishing out for that dumb-looking thing.”

“I wouldn’t be surprised if you became the

man to commission the world's first adaptive muscle car," Alex replied, refusing to let Max's digs get to him. When Max gave him a sour "as if" look in response, Alex put his packet of papers down on the coffee table. "Maybe today isn't the right day for this conversation. I'll just leave the details with you and come back later." Leaving JJ's company felt rather like walking away from the fire on an Arctic expedition, but it was clear the chances of him getting anywhere with Max were thinning fast and it was making him crazy to see her so strained over Max's sour disposition.

"No," JJ said as she shot her brother an almost maternal look that silently shouted *you promised to behave.* "Please don't leave. I really want Max to hear this from you."

"Daxon says meeting you is a monumental mistake." Max threw the assessment out like a dare.

"I don't doubt that." Alex sat back in his chair. "If all you want from us is a boatload of money, it probably is. If you choose to drain every bit of AG's capital in a whopping settlement, that's your right. You'll undoubtedly win and AG will most likely go under and, well, I'll live with it."

"Just like I'm living with this?" Max slapped

one of his legs alarmingly hard. "I'd flinch if I could feel it, but, well…" It was a stunt for shock value. It worked; Alex gulped.

"Max." JJ had gone from annoyed to mortified. "Could we try to do this like adults?"

"Okay, Cushman," Max sat back and crossed his arms. "Win me over."

It was an uphill battle the whole afternoon. Alex found himself exhausted from trying to keep enthusiasm and optimism for Adventure Access in the face of Max's steady resentment. Really, could he blame the man? No matter how one looked at it, poor decisions by Adventure Gear had resulted in Max's injuries. What Alex was asking Max to consider demanded no small amount of maturity, forethought and downright forgiveness. How many men could do that at any age, much less Max's reckless young years?

When JJ suggested a coffee break, Alex was grateful. It was torture being in the same room with JJ and yet unable to speak everything he'd come to Chicago to say. This visit was as much about winning over JJ as it was about gaining Max's partnership—in his heart, convincing JJ was even more important. He'd never jumped at the chance to go brew a pot of coffee with more speed.

Just as they ducked into the alcove that formed Max's kitchen, the apartment's front door opened and Mrs. Jones called a hello. So much for any time alone with JJ. Mrs. Jones headed straight into the kitchen with a pile of fluffy somethings filling up her arms. "Look!"

JJ smiled even as Alex peered at the pile. Sweaters in August? Why would anyone take such delight about sweaters in the middle of the summer?

"The prayer shawls!" JJ ducked over and pulled a red thing from the top of the pile. "Melba found me a red one just like she said." She poked her head around the room divider to call to Max. "Oh, little brother, wait until you see the one Violet made for you—Melba told me all about it. You'll just die when you see it."

"Oh, my goodness, yes!" Mrs. Jones giggled. Evidently she'd seen the whatever-it-was already and found it as amusing as JJ promised. The glimpse of the three of them acting so much like a family—the kidding and hugs and love away from the urgent stress of the hospital rooms—tugged at Alex. His family looked nothing like that now. He wasn't sure it ever had looked anything like this little trio of affection.

Max wheeled into the room, his mouth dropping open when Mrs. Jones unfurled a black knit rectangle with flames licking up from either end—exactly like his wheelchair.

"That is flat-out awesome!" Max marveled, holding out his hands for the thing. "Who made this?"

JJ bent closer to examine the amazing thing, which looked like a cross between a massive black knitted scarf and a hot-rod afghan. "One of the ladies from my friend Melba's Bible study at Gordon Falls Community Church. I told Melba about the paint job on your wheelchair and one of the women came up with the idea. I think they call it a wrap or an afghan when it's for a guy—you'd never use anything called a shawl, that's for sure."

JJ wrapped herself up in the fluffy red shawl and Alex watched the color light up her eyes. She looked so happy. It felt like he never got the chance to see her truly happy. It changed her face in ways that melted his heart and broke it at the same time.

Max was running his fingers through the black, red and orange fringe that trimmed either end of the wrap, as if the flames had grown multicolored tails. "Why'd they do this?"

"Volunteers make them and pray over them." JJ's voice changed to a soft tone Alex hadn't heard in a long time. "The church gives them out to people who need care or comfort or healing. They come in lots of colors, but, Max, I'm pretty sure yours was a custom job."

"People there care about you, Max," said Mrs. Jones, her voice thick with a mother's love. "They all want to see you come back."

Alex could see that Gordon Falls didn't just care about Max Jones. Whether or not JJ had realized it, Gordon Falls had become her home, too. He'd come here, ready to sweep JJ off her feet, to convince her and Max to come to Denver. He'd selfishly made all kinds of plans to graft JJ into his life, forgetting that JJ had made a wonderful new life of her own in Gordon Falls. Now everything was tangled; after watching this, he didn't think he had the heart to ask JJ to consider moving away from Max should he reject the offer. AG was in Denver and Adventure Access could only be in Denver, but it was becoming clear the Jones family shouldn't be uprooted from Gordon Falls. Hadn't he felt the same sense of community even for his short stay there? Could he live with himself if he pulled JJ from the place that had played such an important role in her return to life?

JJ swirled the powder-blue shawl around her

mother's shoulders. They looked so much alike, standing next to each other like that, wrapped in all those fluffy colors. "Aren't they wonderful?" she asked Alex.

The lump in his throat held him as tight as SpiderSilk. He could only nod.

"I'll be back after I have dinner with Alex, Mom." JJ pulled the door to Max's apartment shut and exhaled. The afternoon had been both satisfying and exhausting. Max had waffled from intrigued to defensive to annoyed and just about everything in between.

Alex was trying so hard to engage her brother. The fierceness of his efforts pierced her heart. Alex had nearly broken into a sweat toward the end, focusing every ounce of energy he had into lighting some kind of spark in Max that wasn't just about revenge. Here was the Alex Cushman everyone talked about: the passionate visionary, the man determined to take people to a higher place, a greater adventure. He was nothing short of magnetic, and part of her wanted to take Max and shake him into agreement. A partnership with someone like Alex could change Max's life.

By the end of the afternoon, JJ believed that what Alex proposed could indeed redeem the tragedy that had taken Max's legs away from him. She could actually allow herself to dream that a "Max on Wheels"—as he called himself in his brighter moments—could be a better man than the Max who had walked.

JJ took a moment to stare at her reflection in the polished elevator doors. The woman who looked back at her was so different than the one who stepped off an army transport months ago. This woman was starting to believe in hope. This woman was beginning to believe—in a part of her soul that had been dark and dried up—that Alex Cushman was a gift to her life. The man was such a surging fountain of faith and optimism, it was as if she couldn't help but get doused by what splashed over from his life. It was as true as it was surprising: Alex was a gift from a God she'd convinced herself no longer watched over the Jones family.

The eyes in her reflection said it clearly: *I've lost my heart to Alex Cushman.* It had begun with the impassioned speech way back at Karl's in Gordon Falls. It had grown over the past weeks in the dozens of emails and the delivery of chocolate bars. He'd sent his affections in phone calls, text messages and packages containing AG T-shirts and CDs of ukulele music. A DVD of *White Christmas* that had arrived on her doorstep. Pizzas that appeared on her shifts at the fire department. For a man on the verge of losing his financial footing, he was pulling out all the stops to woo her. In a host of grand and tiny gestures, Alex Cushman had won her heart.

The elevator door slid open to reveal a very impatient Alex. He stood there, hands stuffed in his pockets, looking for all the world like a small boy about to find out whether or not he'd made the varsity team that year.

She didn't know what to tell him. Her emotions—real as they were—were only a small part of a big and complex picture. Denver was far away and Max still needed lots of support. If Max declined Alex's offer, JJ knew she couldn't leave him to fend for himself. Nor could she ignore that Gordon Falls was winning her affections, too. Melba had become a real friend—how long had it been since she'd had true friendships? And what about the guys? GFVFD was becoming a circle of support for her, too. As much as she was coming to feel for Alex, she wasn't yet ready to leave all that behind. Besides, they hadn't even talked about a future together yet. It was far too early for such plans.

"Hello, Bing." The nod to their first meeting wasn't anything she'd planned; it just sort of slipped from the tumble of emotions.

"Hello, Rosemary." She'd half expected some grand Alex-style gesture. Red roses, a ukulele serenade, a snowmaking machine set up on Michigan Avenue to give her Christmas in August. He'd been so persuasive from afar, she'd expected to be swept off their feet once they were in the same room. He'd certainly stared at her during the afternoon's "presentation." Even Max had made some comment about mixed motives. What woman wouldn't be flattered by having someone of Alex's charisma so clearly smitten over her? She'd never seen herself as having that kind of effect on people. Still, he hardly moved. It took her a few seconds for her to realize he was waiting, letting her set the tone.

The man was nearly irresistible, standing there empty-handed and fidgeting like that. Somehow his doubt was more engaging that any dramatic display. "Alex." She sent his name across the air between them, an offering.

His smile was relief and affection and nerves all rolled into one engaging grin. "JJ." Then, shrugging, he tilted his chin up in the direction of Max's apartment. "How'd I do?"

She knew he'd ask. It was clear he'd wanted

to bowl Max over, to walk out of there with Max enthusiastic and signed on. She'd wanted it for him, for Max and maybe even for her, but she was more realistic than that. This might wrap itself up into a happy ending someday, but it wouldn't be simple and it wouldn't be soon. "He didn't toss you out. He's still angry at AG, at *WWW,* pretty much at everyone. I don't know that we could have hoped for much more today."

He *had* hoped for much more—she could see the disappointment in his eyes. "I hadn't realized he was still so angry. I suppose we deserve every bit of it, but wow, a couple of his remarks were like gut punches up there."

Max hadn't bothered to be tactful—that was true. "Max wasn't tactful on two feet, so I don't think we can expect him to be diplomatic on two wheels."

Alex looked at her. "We?"

His doubt surprised her. For a man who so clearly expected to succeed, did he really worry about winning her over? "The latest surveys indicate fifty percent of Joneses are in your corner." Where had such slick and clever language come from? That felt like something she'd chide Alex for saying in a campaign.

Alex furrowed a brow as he opened the

lobby door. "Fifty percent? But there are three of you."

"Mom is still on the fence. She likes the idea of him having a real job, but she hates the idea of him moving to Denver."

"And Max?" He asked the question with an endearing timidity.

"I decided it'd be better if I didn't ask Max what he thought right now. He needs to stew on this for a while before he comes around."

"Hmm." Alex obviously wasn't a man accustomed to ambiguity. It was different than uncertainty, she realized. He made fast and clear decisions, or chose his options, but that wasn't the same thing as having options denied or delayed. Max held many of the cards here, whether he knew it or not.

The night was warm and bright on the Chicago street. It was pretty, in a loud and sparkling kind of way, but JJ felt herself yearning for the quiet glistening of night along the Gordon River. Over the past month, the river had indeed become home. It was a new, comfortable settling in—less surreal than the bubble of wonder she had shared with Alex but definitely home. She had a place in Gordon Falls. Her heart might be broken if Max chose to reject the offer and stay in Chicago, but she'd have a home in which to heal. That felt awful and comforting at the same time. "Where are we going?" she asked to fill the silence with something more than her clamoring thoughts.

"A great little place. I specialize in great little places." He caught her eyes. "And great big ones, too. I made a steak at the bottom of the Grand Canyon that would've knocked your socks off. And this one espresso my Sherpa made me in Tibet, well, it..."

"I believe you." She cut him off, not in the mood to hear what a world figure Alex Cushman was. That wasn't the Alex who'd stolen her heart. The Alex she cared for played bad ukulele and sent doughnuts to small-town firemen. Only he was both those people, and she wasn't yet sure she could deal with that.

They walked the handful of blocks to the restaurant, a charming Italian place filled with snug booths and cozy lighting. Alex had made references to a "near legendary" dating life in Denver—and probably in a dozen other cities around the globe, her doubts added—and it was easy to see why when the maître d' showed them to the nicest, most secluded table in the place.

"The Maxwell Jones portion of today's events has now officially concluded," Alex announced as they slipped into adjoining sides of a red leather V-shaped seat while the waiter adjusted the table between them. "Tonight is all about seeing you again." His voice was low and undramatic. Alex the man, not Alex the visionary. It made her feel better.

After a second's hesitation, he reached for her hand. She smiled and let him take it. "I have really wanted to see you again." His eyes took her back to the dock, back when life wasn't the mess of complications it was now. "Ask Doc—I made him nuts waiting for you to invite me back here."

"I know." It was fun to surprise him, to finally know something he didn't.

"You know?"

"When a Mario Dovini called me about a week ago, it took me a minute or two to work out who he was. Doc pleaded your case pretty eloquently." She shook her head, remembering the man's flowery romantic speech. "Actually, he was even hokier than you described him. Somehow, though, the guy manages to pull it off."

Alex actually flushed. "It's the accent. All the Italian tones and consonants let Doc get away with saying the most outrageous things."

He pursed his lips and raised his eyebrows in an inquisitive sort of wince. "What'd he say?"

JJ wasn't sure she could repeat the Italian's hopelessly gooey pleas. She felt her own cheeks redden a bit. "He said, among other things—" she looked down at the crisp white napkin, needing to duck out of the heat of Alex's eyes "—that Max Jones wasn't the only man in my life who'd fallen hard and would never be the same."

Alex dropped his head into one hand. "That's truly awful." After a second, he returned his gaze to her. "Would I compound it by saying it's awfully true?"

JJ couldn't help but roll her eyes at that one.

"I missed that most of all." His face was close to hers, and when she made herself look up, his eyes were so full of emotion it was hard to breathe. "How I can love you most for the way you roll your eyes is so beyond me."

JJ couldn't reply. It was as if every part of her body had stopped working except her heart, which was pounding unbearably at the moment.

"It's true." He grabbed both of her hands. "I don't really know how, but I have completely fallen for you, JJ. This whole thing should be awful, should be filled with pain and heartbreak—and it is, lots of it is—but I also know that I wouldn't take back meeting you for all the success in the world. I'm right where I'm supposed to be, doing right what it is I'm supposed to be doing. I've never been able to stand and hold the line on anything in my life ever before this. But you managed to teach me how. You stood there and held the line. In the war. With Max. With the fire department. With me. I kept looking for places to escape to, and every time I'd try I'd turn around and you'd still be there. You taught me how to stand firm. And…and I love you for it."

He loved her. She'd known on some level for weeks, the way he was pursuing her, but to hear him say it was so powerful. Someone like Alex Cushman, who could probably have any woman in the world he chose, loved *her.* Beaten down, unglamorous, stubborn, argumentative her. What was more, he loved her *for* those qualities, not in spite of them. JJ fought the urge to shake her head and blink because it seemed impossible that what he'd said was real.

Alex's hands tightened on hers. "Please… say something." He was nearly frantic. To have someone yearn for her heart that badly was overwhelming. She wanted to cry and laugh and whoop and fall over in a dead faint all at once.

"I love you back." No, that was the wrong way to say it. JJ squinted her eyes shut, embarrassed by her own clumsy words. Then she felt Alex's hands on her face as he planted a small kiss on each of her eyelids. The gesture was so sweet and tender that any resistance she'd had burst into a thousand sparkling pieces. She opened her eyes and spent an infinite moment gazing into the endless blue of his eyes before he kissed her. True and full, deep and soft, his kiss was beyond any description her workaday vocabulary could ever contain.

He pulled away just far enough to let their foreheads touch, and JJ felt rather than saw his smile. "Whoa."

"I love you, too. That's how you're supposed to say it."

"Nah, I like your way much better." He kissed her again, and JJ let herself revel in the happiness of it. Honestly, she didn't think she'd ever get to be this happy again. Somehow, since the war, she'd talked herself into thinking "not such a mess" was the most she could hope to achieve. "I am so very, very glad you love me back." Alex's words were warm and brilliant, nearly humming with energy. "I don't think even Doc could describe how glad I am you love me back."

"What if it's not enough?" She hated that the doubt poked its ugly head into the moment before she could stop it.

It didn't faze him. One finger traced her brow as if to wipe away the furrow. "I think it is. I think love is always enough." He smiled as she tried—unsuccessfully—not to roll her eyes. "I'm not saying it won't be complicated. It's already complicated." His smile widened, warm and dashing. "But it just got a whole lot better."

She wasn't the full-out optimist he was. "You're there and I'm here and…"

"No." He put a finger to her lips. "I'm right here and you're right here. Everything else is just an obstacle in need of a solution."

"I want to believe you."

"Then believe me. Believe that God wouldn't pull our hearts together for no reason. Believe that it can work out, that He can work it out, even if we can't see that now. Believe in Christmas in July, just for tonight."

She could do that. Looking into his eyes made her feel as if she could do anything. "I can't believe I'm in love with you." It was almost too wondrous to be true.

"Hey." He pulled back in mock indignation. "Why the surprise? I happen to be very lovable.

I made *Backpack Magazine*'s most eligible bachelor list of two-thousand-and-I can't-remember."

JJ found herself scowling and grinning like a fool at the same time. It felt downright splendid. "You made that up."

He planted his chin in one hand and just gazed at her. Gazed as if she were the most amazing thing he'd ever seen. For so long she thought she'd turn as red as the fire trucks back in Gordon Falls. "I love you back, JJ Jones. And we'll make it work. Well, us and the Almighty. I think we'll need a hefty dose of divine intervention on this one."

The words didn't ring false. Not a bit. With a startled little glow somewhere way down deep, JJ discovered she still believed in divine intervention. God hadn't turned His back. And that meant anything was possible. In that moment, JJ Jones became the tiniest of optimists.

It felt delightful.

Chapter Eighteen

Max had spent all morning with Tony Daxon and it was making JJ crazy. Part of her wanted to stay in Chicago and sit in on the meeting, but Max wouldn't have it. Perhaps it was better she was back in Gordon Falls today, going over the paperwork for the fall cabin season.

She'd spent the entire train ride back in a romantic fog. Alex's final good-night kiss back in the lobby of Max's apartment had left her breathless, and she had been grateful she'd had the elevator ride up to Max's floor to compose herself. Not that Max or Mom cared—they were knee-deep in an argument over the last physical therapist Max had "fired." Some days it seemed like Max took his anger out on everything within reach.

It was good Max's boat-rental employees

were out of that reach; they were outstanding at keeping things going without much oversight. JJ had expected to spend the morning "putting out fires" in the figurative sense instead of the literal sense, but even for the cottages it had mostly been routine management. Something Alex probably could have done blindfolded. This must be what love was like—it was almost teenagerish how everything made her think of him. He'd gone back to Denver, giving Max time and space to ponder his offer to join Adventure Access. That was a smart idea, but having him so far away produced a constant gnawing ache in her chest.

How, Lord, how could we ever make this work? The prayer came out of her without decision or effort—the way prayers used to. *Why slam our lives together when they can't really mesh? Why draw me so strongly to Gordon Falls now when it would be so much better if I could go to Denver with Max?*

As she updated the rental calendar and paid bills, the soldier/strategist in her kept concocting scenarios and outcomes. Stay in Gordon Falls. Go to Denver. Max says yes and goes to Adventure Access. Max says no and stays here. Max sues and loses and spirals downward. Max sues and wins and spirals out of control. There were just too many variables—all with enough pros and cons to obscure any clear choice.

After settling the last file, JJ checked her watch and saw that she had two hours before her shift at the firehouse. Needing to grab some additional peace, JJ opted for something she hadn't done since coming to Gordon Falls: she "rented" one of Max's canoes and went out on the water.

Sitting in the canoe, hearing the water lap gently against the side, JJ felt the river do its wonders. Chief Bradens had a boat—one that used to belong to Max, actually—called The Escape Clause. He said he used it to come out on the water and get his head straight. Looking back at Gordon Falls, JJ could see how that worked. There was something about the perspective from out here—clarity she couldn't seem to reach on shore. *You know where my home should be, don't You, Lord? I look at this place and it feels like home. A huge part of me wants to stay. Only now my heart has found a home in a man who isn't here. And I can't help but think that's Your doing.*

She felt the current tug the boat in one direction, making her work harder to go the other. Wasn't that what was happening to her now?

Fighting a current she couldn't see to a place she couldn't guess? *You've laid out events I could never have imagined. I used to be able to trust You in that. How do I learn to trust You for the rest of this?* The more JJ thought about it, trust wasn't really a skill one could learn. You either trusted your team in the army or you didn't; it was a choice. *I could choose to trust You, couldn't I? I love Max and want what's best for him. I know I'm in Gordon Falls for a reason—at least for now. And I love Alex, but his life is elsewhere.*

She laughed at her declaration. Didn't God already know all this? Hadn't He known the whole time—even before she'd realized she loved Alex Cushman? Suddenly, out of nowhere, her brain recalled the favorite saying of the army chaplain that had helped her grieve for Angie Carlisle: "Pray for calm but row for shore." Ridiculous advice to give a distraught woman in the middle of a desert, but she knew what it meant: do what you can where you are and trust God with the rest.

She was a firefighter here in Gordon Falls. She was Max's sister. She was a woman in love with Alex Cushman. God would have to take all that and make calm. She would have to row for shore.

* * *

Alex had to give Max one thing: the guy had a natural flare for the dramatic. His email said it all, point blank: "No. I'm staying here."

If it had been a piece of paper, Alex would have crumpled it up and thrown it against the wall. As it was, all he could do was slam down the lid of his laptop hard enough to make Doc look up from the harness he was testing.

"No," he growled, standing up to pace behind his desk. Failure wasn't the kind of thing that could just be walked off like a leg cramp, but he couldn't sit still while the weight of this crashed down on him.

"No, what?" Doc's face showed the question to be unnecessary, more like a last-ditch hope that the decline was for something else.

"Max turned me down. He's going to stay in Chicago and sue us into oblivion." That was overdramatic, but he wasn't feeling reasonable right now. "I know he should be on our team. I know we could do great things if we could just get him out here."

"So you know just what will fix Max Jones's life, do you?" Doc's raised eyebrow poked an annoying hole in Alex's conscience.

"Yes! No. I mean, I *feel* it—that it's right.

I've never had an idea plant itself in my head with more certainty. This is the answer."

Doc put down the tool he was using. "This is *your* answer. Max just gave you his."

Alex knew Doc was right, but the failure of it all seemed to choke him right now. He wanted to push back, to argue with Doc, but found he couldn't. "It's just that there's no solution now. Everybody loses." *Everybody loses.* The words clanged around his head like a loose gear.

"Everybody loses *what,* exactly?"

"Everybody loses…everything. We lose Adventure Gear, Max loses a chance at a new career, we lose the chance to make this right, you probably lose your job, I've already lost Sam…" Alex glared at Doc. "Want me to go on?"

Doc sat back against his worktable. "As a matter of fact, I do. You're missing something important on that list."

Alex shot the Italian his darkest "I'm in no mood to play games" glare.

Doc sighed. "What does your Josephine lose? You are making this all about Max, and that's wrong. A lot of it is about Max Jones—as it should be—but it also has to be about you. And about you and your Josephine."

Alex felt his jaw drop. "When in the world did you start calling her Josephine?"

Doc shook his head. "Americans. You take a lovely name like Josephine and you chop it up into letters. I cannot call a beautiful woman JJ. How can you call the woman you care about by such a thing?"

Alex fought the urge to snarl, "You're kidding me, right?" but it was useless to have such arguments with Doc. He was who he was. Instead, Alex wiped his hands down his face and said, "The beautiful woman in question *likes* to be called JJ and doesn't like to be called Josephine, that's why."

"I asked what JJ stood for and she told me. I asked her permission to use such a beautiful name for a beautiful woman and she said that I could."

Doc's smug smile sank into Alex's gut. "Sure, when you put it *that* way."

Doc picked his tool back up. "Which I did. And you have not answered my question. Yes, you've lost Samuel, but that would have happened in any case. What do you lose now?"

Alex's brain kept shouting "everything," but he forced his thoughts past the frustration to reach for the answer. "JJ," he said finally, sinking into his chair. "I think I lose JJ. I know she would have come to Denver with Max, or I could have persuaded her to come eventually.

But now I don't think she will. I'm not sure I could ask her to."

Doc twisted a piece of harness, trimming one end. "Do you believe Max is the only man who could do this job?"

Alex had to think. "I believe he is *the* man for the job. He is the man who is supposed to have the job. But could someone else fill that role? Doc, I have no idea. It's supposed to be Max. I can't explain it any other way."

"And Max will not come to Denver."

Alex spun in his desk chair, wanting this conversation to be over. "Nope."

"And your Josephine, she will not come to Denver."

"Not without Max, and maybe not at all." What, was Doc determined to make him repeat all the day's worst news?

"And there is no solution."

"Not that I can see." Alex wanted to bang his head on the desk.

"Then you are not the Alexander I know." Doc started to laugh, which just doubled Alex's annoyance. "Finding solutions where no one else could was always your gift. And now I can see the solution and you cannot? The world has become a funny place."

"What?" Doc only laughed, which made

Alex want to tromp over there and take his tools away until the infuriating Italian quit his guessing games. *"What?"*

Doc silently went back to work. What's worse, he started to whistle.

"You are the most…" Alex simply grabbed his car keys before he said something he'd regret. "I'm out of here. It's been a bad enough day already without you adding to it."

Alex stomped from the room, stalking down the hall in a wave of fury and frustration. He was almost to the front door when it hit him like an avalanche. It was so simple, so drastic, so obvious, Alex couldn't fathom how he'd missed it. He turned around so fast he nearly fell over, and sprinted back to yank the office door open with so much force it banged into the wall. Alex darted over to Doc's worktable and planted his hands atop the rigging. "Move."

Doc looked up as if nothing unusual had just happened.

"If JJ and Max won't come to Adventure Access, I'll take Adventure Access to them. We'll move the whole shebang to Chicago, or Gordon Falls or wherever near there that fits. Everybody wins."

Doc offered a tilted smile. "Not everyone."

"You wouldn't come? You *have* to come. I

think I can do this without Sam, but I *know* I can't do this without you."

"I'll come. But only if you move for you, or for her and not lay everything at that poor young man's feet. *Your* life is not *his* to save, even if you think *you're* saving his."

It would have been the most pretentious, overly dramatic thing to say—had it not been absolutely right. Still, that was Doc. He always knew what was truly wrong, even when no one else could see it.

Alex grabbed the dear man by his shoulder. "Doc, if you'll excuse me, I've got a plane to catch."

Doc's smile filled the room. "You always do."

The engine pulled into the bay and JJ swung down off her position, tired and sweaty. The garage fire had been stubborn, but the brigade had worked together well to contain it. The past two calls proved she'd become a member of the team. As she undid the fastenings on her bunker coat, Wally nudged her shoulder and pointed. "What's with him again?"

"Who?" JJ turned to see Alex standing in the wide driveway. Her heart did a teenager-worthy flip at the sight of him. Max had declared his decision, and now she didn't know what lay ahead for her and Alex. Something in his eyes, however, told her he'd come up with something—Alex was practically buzzing with excitement. Despite the grime and her cumbersome gear, JJ walked over to where he was.

"You're beautiful." The truth was she smelled like smoke and gasoline and two hours of exertion, not to mention her sweaty hair and sooty everything. Not the standard definition of beauty by any means, but Alex's eyes displayed a full-out smitten adoration that made her cheeks redden.

"You're here." Would this be how it went from now on? Stretches of settling in while missing him punctuated by sudden appearances that would startle her heart?

"I'm here. I need to talk to you."

JJ shucked out of the thick coat. "I can't change Max's mind. I've tried." She had. Half of her truly wanted Alex's plan to work out, to transplant Max into a new life and all of them to Denver. The other half recognized how much Gordon Falls already meant to him and was coming to mean for her. Max was finally thinking of one place as home, and that was worth so much. She just didn't know if it was worth losing her chance with Alex.

"It's not about Max." He shrugged. "Okay, maybe it's a bit about Max, but not really. That doesn't make any sense, does it?" He shut his eyes for a second. "How fast can you get out of here?"

"Not fast. The shift's almost over but we've got to clean up and there's paperwork and..."

Chief Bradens appeared behind her from out of nowhere. "And I think we can have her out of here in ten minutes unless she has to put on makeup and do her hair, which will cost you another thirty."

JJ spun around. "Chief, I..."

He smirked. "So I'm a softy. Deal with it. The guy bought us doughnuts. And pizza."

She gaped at her boss, unable to come up with the right answer for the situation. In response, he merely checked his watch, gave Alex an exaggerated wink and walked away. JJ took one last look over her shoulder, held up one hand to Alex and managed to choke out, "I'll be back in fifteen.

"Ten," he countered, absurdly impatient.

"Fifteen." She held her ground. "I need a shower."

When she returned after the fastest postincineration shower in GFVFD history, Alex hadn't moved from his spot in the driveway.

The guys found this hilarious and made all kinds of comments to her as she walked out of the bay to meet him, at which point Alex greeted her with an enormous kiss despite—or perhaps because of—the raucous audience. Whistles and whoops and one call of "Way to go, doughnut man!" echoed in the large engine bay behind her until JJ was sure she was the color of the truck.

"Can we get out of here now?" She laughed into his neck when he wouldn't stop covering her in small kisses. It startled her—in the nicest of ways—how she could let him be so affectionate given the totally uncertain nature of their relationship. Maybe because he exuded certainty, that solidness of purpose that made him able to launch companies out of disasters. With or without Max, she had no doubt Alex Cushman would turn Adventure Access into something the world had never seen before.

Alex walked quickly, trying hard to hold in whatever it was he came to say. His passion for life, his vitality, seeped into her whenever they were together. Maybe that was why she missed him so much when he was gone. In half a block his impatience got the best of him and he turned to take her by both shoulders. "I'm moving here. I'm going to pick up the pieces of what used to be AG and move the whole operation here."

"But..."

"There is no AG or Adventure Access without me. And there is no me without you. It's so simple I don't know how I couldn't see it earlier."

"Because it's not so simple. All those people, all those jobs you were trying to save..."

"The ones who matter will come along. And we'll partner with the rehabilitation hospital for others. I built a company from the ground up in Denver, so I can build one in Chicago. Or right here. Or someplace in between. Because you belong here and I, well, I used to belong everywhere in the world but now I only belong in one place. And that's here with you."

JJ tried to take in the enormity of what he was saying. "You're moving your company here to be with me."

"Unless you know some way to pick up all of Gordon Falls and move it to Denver. But that wouldn't work either because I need it to be here. *I* need to be here. I can't guarantee I won't have to travel now and—"

She cut him off with a kiss that let loose her whole heart for the first time in her life. Her whole, healed heart. Tony Daxon had been wrong; she wouldn't have to choose where her loyalties lay. God had given her a whole, healed life where, in true Alex Cushman fashion, everybody won.

"Wow," Alex exclaimed softly, no less stunned than she. "If I had known a little relocation would bring that out in you, I'd have moved a month ago."

JJ let her head fall against his shoulder. "No, you wouldn't have. Not until you were sure you'd found the solution. That's what I love about you, Alex—you never give up."

He brought her hand up and kissed it. A grandly elegant gesture to a woman in jeans, wet hair and a GFVFD T-shirt. "I couldn't give up on us. Even if I wanted to—which I absolutely did not. It just took me a while to work it all out. If there's anyone who doesn't give up, it's God trying to get an idea through my thick skull."

She turned her head to look up into his eyes. How perfect it felt to be in his arms. How safe and whole. "Speaking of thick skulls, what about Max?"

"I'm hoping he'll say yes now that he can stay here." He sighed. "I really think he's the guy to bring into Adventure Access. We'll still stand by any settlement that comes down, regardless, but I still think we have more than just money to offer him. I've decided it might be best to trust that God has someone else in mind if Max says no." Alex put his arm around JJ's shoulder and began walking with something close to a swagger. "Who knows? Maybe he's not quite ready for a family business. Studies show it takes a certain personality to work with relatives, and I know how badly it can turn sour."

JJ stopped walking and stared at him. Did he just say what she thought he'd said? "Relatives?"

"Well, in six months when we're ready to take Max on, I figure you'll definitely have succumbed to my legendary charms and said yes."

Every ounce of calm left her body. "Yes to *what?*"

His smile was nothing short of gleaming. "You don't think I'm going to let you in on that now, do you? These things take time to do well. An Amazonian chief once told me I was a veritable fountain of patience."

JJ applied a mock scowl. "And some chief once told you that you had the soul of a monkey. I didn't believe that, either."

Alex started walking, chin up, smug as could be. "Nope. No spoilers. But you're smart, so you can guess what it might be. You'll never get it out of me until the time is right."

JJ caught him by the arm and kissed him for all she was worth. For all *he* was worth. For all the two of them could do together, right here in Gordon Falls. She took no small amount of pride in rendering him momentarily speechless.

"Wow," he said, his voice gruff. "Maybe you will get it out of me sooner than that."

She chuckled, loving how light the world felt right now. "Can I be the one to tell Max?"

That surprised him. "You? Really?"

"Well, the two of us together. I want the chance to give him some happy news. And even though you are Mr. Persuasion, I think maybe I can help him see how good Adventure Access would be for him."

"I imagine you could." His smile made her heart pound. "I love you, you know that?"

"I love you back." And this time, it didn't feel at all wrong to put it that way.

Epilogue

The antique paddle wheel steamboat was decked out almost beyond recognition in white-and-red bunting. Alex stood at the edge of the dock trying to breathe. In seconds, JJ would come down the path and join him and the guests gathered there. They'd board the boat as Alex and JJ, but they'd step off as Mr. and Mrs. Alexander Cushman.

He loved that JJ insisted they get married on the river, even though the late April date made for risky weather. God had smiled on their plans—today was clear and bright with just the perfect bit of briskness. Doc put a hand on Alex's shoulder as the sound of sirens echoed across the way. The Gordon Falls Volunteer Fire Department had insisted on delivering JJ to the wedding in dramatic style.

The gathered guests broke out in applause as

a fire truck, decked out as ceremoniously as the boat, pulled into view. He caught a glimpse of white fluff inside the cab and he saw a wave of JJ's hand, but nothing prepared him for the vision of her stepping out onto the path. His bride was breathtaking. No vista on earth could compare to the sight of her standing there in the brilliant April sunshine, smiling at him for all the world to see.

A second later, Max rolled up beside JJ, and she placed her hand on the back of his chair just as tenderly as any bride takes her father's elbow. Max cut a pretty fine figure in his tux, not to mention the pinstripes done up on his wheels for the occasion. One of his first projects at Adventure Access had been a series of customizable wheel placards for the company's off-road wheelchair line. "Maxing out" had become a company catchphrase for tricking out equipment, and Alex couldn't have been happier to adopt the term.

"Ready to welcome your bride aboard?" Pastor Allen said with a wide smile.

"Absolutely. Will you look at that woman? That beauty is gonna be Mrs. Cushman the next time she steps on land."

The ceremony was a blur of joy as Alex watched himself place the ring on JJ's hand.

"Now we start the greatest adventure of their lives," he whispered after they kissed, "with this." At that moment, the steamboat whistle announced man and wife to the whole wide world. He thought that would be the most unusual touch of the celebration until the captain called for the bride and groom to take their first dance.

None of the guests would understand the band's orders to break into "White Christmas" in the middle of April, but he knew why. Now it was the new Mrs. Cushman who was the source of brilliant creative ideas. Everybody won.

* * * * *

Dear Reader,

We all fall down. Some of us physically, some of us emotionally, some of us figuratively. As someone wise once said, “It’s the getting back up that matters.” It’s a fallen world, and we are surrounded by people trying to get back up. Most times we’re just trying to get back up on our own two feet ourselves, aren’t we? God often sends us a lifeline, but frequently it isn’t in the shape, form or person we expected. That’s because the Author of our faith knows, even better than we do, what’s truly needed. I hope that JJ and Alex’s story gives you “hope at the end of your rope.” God can always be counted on to heal, to equip and to restore. As always, feel free to contact me at www.alliepleiter.com or P.O. Box 7026, Villa Park, IL, 60181—I’d love to hear from you!

Questions for Discussion

1. Would you have gone out on the dock to see who was there? Why or why not?

2. Alex says, "I'm trying to figure out why it doesn't all fit together anymore and what to do about it." Have you ever felt like that? What happened?

3. The nurse tells JJ to remember to let people help her in her crisis. Do you have trouble accepting help in a crisis? Why or why not?

4. Is JJ right or wrong to blame Alex for his involvement in the accident?

5. Alex says, "There's no way to make this right, ever." Have you ever found yourself feeling like that? What did you do?

6. How is your relationship with your sibling, if you have one? Is it strained or strong?

7. Alex says, "I can't…not…help even though I don't see how I *can* help." Has there ever been a situation where you felt you had to help but didn't know how?

8. Is there an insomniac in your life? How do they deal with it?

9. JJ says she no longer believes life is supposed to be fair. Do you agree or disagree?

10. What are your feelings about pranks like the ones at the firehouse? Are they good for bonding or mean chances for things to get out of hand?

11. Have you ever had a battle that you could fight *with* someone but not *for* them? What did you learn?

12. Alex says he's been all around the world but his time on the Gordon River was the best vacation he's ever had. What was your favorite vacation and why?

13. Have you had a "radical, drastic opportunity" in your life? What came from it?

14. JJ says that "there's a huge difference between losing and surrender." Do you agree?

15. JJ says trust is a choice to be made, not a skill to be learned. Where has that been true in your life?

LARGER-PRINT BOOKS!

GET 2 FREE LARGER-PRINT NOVELS PLUS 2 FREE MYSTERY GIFTS

Love Inspired®

Larger-print novels are now available...

YES! Please send me 2 FREE LARGER-PRINT Love Inspired® novels and my 2 FREE mystery gifts (gifts are worth about $10). After receiving them, if I don't wish to receive any more books, I can return the shipping statement marked "cancel." If I don't cancel, I will receive 6 brand-new novels every month and be billed just $5.24 per book in the U.S. or $5.74 per book in Canada. That's a savings of at least 23% off the cover price. It's quite a bargain! Shipping and handling is just 50¢ per book in the U.S. and 75¢ per book in Canada.* I understand that accepting the 2 free books and gifts places me under no obligation to buy anything. I can always return a shipment and cancel at any time. Even if I never buy another book, the two free books and gifts are mine to keep forever.

122/322 IDN F49Y

Name (PLEASE PRINT)

Address Apt. #

City State/Prov. Zip/Postal Code

Signature (if under 18, a parent or guardian must sign)

Mail to the **Harlequin® Reader Service:**
IN U.S.A.: P.O. Box 1867, Buffalo, NY 14240-1867
IN CANADA: P.O. Box 609, Fort Erie, Ontario L2A 5X3

Are you a current subscriber to Love Inspired books and want to receive the larger-print edition?
Call 1-800-873-8635 or visit www.ReaderService.com.

* Terms and prices subject to change without notice. Prices do not include applicable taxes. Sales tax applicable in N.Y. Canadian residents will be charged applicable taxes. Offer not valid in Quebec. This offer is limited to one order per household. Not valid for current subscribers to Love Inspired Larger-Print books. All orders subject to credit approval. Credit or debit balances in a customer's account(s) may be offset by any other outstanding balance owed by or to the customer. Please allow 4 to 6 weeks for delivery. Offer available while quantities last.

Your Privacy—The Harlequin® Reader Service is committed to protecting your privacy. Our Privacy Policy is available online at www.ReaderService.com or upon request from the Harlequin Reader Service.

We make a portion of our mailing list available to reputable third parties that offer products we believe may interest you. If you prefer that we not exchange your name with third parties, or if you wish to clarify or modify your communication preferences, please visit us at www.ReaderService.com/consumerschoice or write to us at Harlequin Reader Service Preference Service, P.O. Box 9062, Buffalo, NY 14269. Include your complete name and address.

LILPDIR13R

ReaderService.com

Manage your account online!

- Review your order history
- Manage your payments
- Update your address

We've designed the Harlequin® Reader Service website just for you.

Enjoy all the features!

- Reader excerpts from any series
- Respond to mailings and special monthly offers
- Discover new series available to you
- Browse the Bonus Bucks catalog
- Share your feedback

Visit us at:

ReaderService.com

RS13

LARGER-PRINT BOOKS!

GET 2 FREE LARGER-PRINT NOVELS PLUS 2 FREE MYSTERY GIFTS

Love Inspired® SUSPENSE
RIVETING INSPIRATIONAL ROMANCE

Larger-print novels are now available...

YES! Please send me 2 FREE LARGER-PRINT Love Inspired® Suspense novels and my 2 FREE mystery gifts (gifts are worth about $10). After receiving them, if I don't wish to receive any more books, I can return the shipping statement marked "cancel." If I don't cancel, I will receive 4 brand-new novels every month and be billed just $5.24 per book in the U.S. or $5.74 per book in Canada. That's a savings of at least 23% off the cover price. It's quite a bargain! Shipping and handling is just 50¢ per book in the U.S. and 75¢ per book in Canada.* I understand that accepting the 2 free books and gifts places me under no obligation to buy anything. I can always return a shipment and cancel at any time. Even if I never buy another book, the two free books and gifts are mine to keep forever.

110/310 IDN F5CC

Name (PLEASE PRINT)

Address Apt. #

City State/Prov. Zip/Postal Code

Signature (if under 18, a parent or guardian must sign)

Mail to the **Harlequin® Reader Service:**
IN U.S.A.: P.O. Box 1867, Buffalo, NY 14240-1867
IN CANADA: P.O. Box 609, Fort Erie, Ontario L2A 5X3

Are you a current subscriber to Love Inspired Suspense books and want to receive the larger-print edition? Call 1-800-873-8635 or visit www.ReaderService.com.

* Terms and prices subject to change without notice. Prices do not include applicable taxes. Sales tax applicable in N.Y. Canadian residents will be charged applicable taxes. Offer not valid in Quebec. This offer is limited to one order per household. Not valid for current subscribers to Love Inspired Suspense larger-print books. All orders subject to credit approval. Credit or debit balances in a customer's account(s) may be offset by any other outstanding balance owed by or to the customer. Please allow 4 to 6 weeks for delivery. Offer available while quantities last.

Your Privacy—The Harlequin® Reader Service is committed to protecting your privacy. Our Privacy Policy is available online at www.ReaderService.com or upon request from the Harlequin Reader Service.

We make a portion of our mailing list available to reputable third parties that offer products we believe may interest you. If you prefer that we not exchange your name with third parties, or if you wish to clarify or modify your communication preferences, please visit us at www.ReaderService.com/consumerschoice or write to us at Harlequin Reader Service Preference Service, P.O. Box 9062, Buffalo, NY 14269. Include your complete name and address.

LISLPDIR13R